THE BARON AT BISHOPS AVENUE

Jason Blacker

ISBN-13: 978-1-927623-56-5

For my mother who taught me all about justice and fairness.

CHAPTER ONE

House of Lords

THE Palace of Westminster is one of the iconic buildings of the United Kingdom and specifically the City of London. Indeed, most of the world knows the Elizabeth Tower and the iconic clock at the top of such tower called colloquially "Big Ben". Though the clock is not named. Big Ben refers to the largest of the five bells in the belfry, and the only bell that rings in the hours. But that aside, perhaps what is less well known is that both Houses of Parliament sit their sessions at Westminster Palace. This is the House of Commons and the upper house is known as the House of Lords.

For some odd reason Westminster Palace always reminded Eric Marmalade of dragon's teeth. Perhaps it was all the pointed spires or the architectural design. Though on more dour days like today Eric felt that the metaphor of the Houses of Parliament looking more like dragon's teeth had more to do with the bickering that took place in the Lords Chamber than with any actual aesthetic of the building's design.

The fifteenth of November in 1920 was a Monday. A Monday that Eric was not thrilled about to be attending the Lords Chamber. There wasn't anything specifically disastrous about this day, rather it was a day of disappointment like many hundreds that had preceded it.

Eric had always considered himself staunchly liberal. But for the past few years he had been sitting opposite the Woolsack. He was now known as a "crossbencher". The word was spat out as if it were distasteful. It was a slur really. And one to which Eric didn't take too kindly. But here he was, a crossbencher, having found himself without a political party to follow since Herbert Henry Asquith had been defeated by the current Prime Minister David Lloyd George. This was the problem with politics, it had less to do with ideology and more to do with emotionality. And for the last little while Asquith and Lloyd George had been fighting about ideology when in reality they just didn't like each other.

If Eric were to choose sides, he might have sided with Lloyd George. But in fairness, he practically disliked them equally. They were quarrelsome and power hungry. The reason the Liberal Party had forked into two was because Asquith had sought a Conservative coalition for he lacked the courage to stand by liberal principles. Though to be fair to him, Eric wondered if his liberal principles were of convenience. He was a womanizer and arrogant leader thinking ever more of himself for having become the longest serving Prime Minister England had endured. And an endurance it was.

Nevertheless, the conservatives were no better and the National Liberal Party under Lloyd George only slightly more playable to Eric's tastes. Indeed, as Eric stepped into the Lords Chamber he wondered why he did so. Perhaps it was some archaic sort of honor that he was here in fact to serve the greater good of England and her people. Though he oftentimes thought he might be fooling himself.

The dull hum of the place was reminiscent of a hornet's nest. An idea that was not far off. Eric sat down in the front row reserved for the crossbenchers. All around him sat mostly rotund, older white men on the plump red cushions of the benches. In front of him, across a large desk and chaise lounge about fifty feet away sat the Lord Chancellor, Baron Christopher Marphallow, on his Woolsack. He was a fat, short man. Five feet six inches on a good day and almost as wide as he was tall. He looked younger than his fifty seven years thanks to the fat in his jowls and chin. His eyes were squinty and his voice was hoarse and staccato as he gasped for breath between every thought. He had a thin wispy mustache that drooped like miniature mammoth tusks from his upper lip. He twirled them for emphasis and when he had nothing to say but wanted a moment to think.

Eric didn't like him. He was a difficult man to like for anyone with any common sense. But he ingratiated himself with the right people and that gave him the position of Lord Chancellor, and an opportunity to sit against the Woolsack cushion.

Eric politely greeted Lord Perry Fernsby. He was an undistinguished looking man of middle age and thinning hair. The only problem was that he didn't know it. Or chose to cover it up. He had grown the hair on his left side long enough to comb over his thinning pate. He had a full beard well kept. Perhaps to keep your eyes off his thinning head. He was average in every way. A quite dull and boring man. An example of the reason why Eric could no longer consider himself a supporter of hereditary peerage.

To Eric's right was Lord Larmer Loughty. A tall thin man who had spent a lifetime ducking under doors. As such, his carriage was stooped and he wore a permanently furrowed brow across his pale white forehead. His eyes were a diluted blue and his hair, thin only in diameter, covered his head and his face held no hint of hair other than wispy eyebrows that seemed surprised to have arisen above his eyes.

"You look happy to be here," said Lord Loughty as he smiled at Eric.

Eric grinned at him.

"Is it that obvious?" he asked.

Larmer nodded and looked over at the Lord Chancellor who had stood and was getting ready to address the House of Lords. The hum turned to a murmur and then the chamber fell silent.

"My Lords," said Baron Marphallow, looking around and taking a moment to breathe, "Lord Huppington has been granted the right to speak first."

Marphallow looked over at the Government's Bench and nodded at a young man in his early forties with a very round face, greying hair and ruddy complexion. This was Lord Percivil Huppington. His two eyes were squeezed together on either side of his nose. A small nose that wasn't much more than a red lump of putty squashed into the middle of his face. He stood up and looked around. He didn't say anything for a moment, smiling benevolently as if he were the king overlooking his loyal subjects. He then looked at a wheezing Marphallow lying against the Woolsack like a beached sea lion.

"Thank you, Lord Chancellor," said Huppington before turning to look across at the Opposition's Bench. "My Lords, I fear I must once again declare my utter opposition to England's decision to rename British East Africa. Are we not talking about British lands? Indeed, the land that God has given great England to shower with civilization and the Englishman's benevolence. Is not calling British East Africa, Kenya, a slap against the strength of our empire?"

Huppington was becoming droned out by boos and hisses from the opposition. Before he could carry on, Lord Sinjin Paussage stood up to berate him.

"My Lords," he said forcefully, "is it not time to move on? British East Africa is now Kenya and the government has agreed on such. Lord Huppington wastes our time by wishing to discuss this matter which many months ago had already been put to rest."

Paussage was a forceful speaker. A well known drinker with the purpled dimpled nose to show for it, he was nonetheless eloquent when he so chose to be. A fat man with a bald head, he could be an imposing figure if you were not on his side. He sat down to an echo of "here, heres" and polite applause. Huppington remained unaffected.

He started to orate again about his displeasure regarding the renaming. Eric turned a deaf ear to him. He was an ignorant and generally facile man with little depth beyond his immediate interest. Eric couldn't care less what a country was called, and the fact that black Africans were being governed by outsiders from thousands of miles away didn't bring him comfort. He knew that it was only a matter of time until the African would demand to govern Africa. He had seen the horrors of war first hand in South Africa. And he had felt the distrust of the African during his tenure there. In any event, he had little interest in Africa as he had little business there. But as a humanitarian he could easily see the calamity brewing against the backdrop of the future like storm clouds gathering their cavalry.

Eric sighed. It was a soft inaudible sigh. He shouldn't have come in today to the Lords Chamber. It was off to a terrible start. He looked at his fingers and he looked at the backs of his hands. He was forty two and now middle aged. His hands were starting to show it. He kept trim and healthy but the skin was getting noticeably thinner. Eric's mind was not present as he could still subconsciously hear the droning of Huppington. To his right, movement stirred him from his reverie. Lord Loughty had stood.

"If it please my lords," he said, his voice carrying over the top of Huppington's, "I'd like to bring our attention to more pressing matters."

Loughty stood as he let the ebb of cheers wash over him. Marphallow took his time standing, and dabbed at his brow with his handkerchief. The effort of merely rising was a rousing event for him.

"I allow Lord Loughty the floor," said Marphallow as he turned to Huppington. "If the Lord of the Government's Bench will kindly take a seat."

Huppington threw his arms up in disgust. But it was a half-hearted effort. He knew he was defeated. If nothing else, he just liked to hear himself talk. And talk at length.

Marphallow nodded at Loughty and sat down slowly as if worried someone had stuffed the

Woolsack with pins.

"Thank you, Lord Chancellor," said Loughty. "Notwithstanding my noble friend's assertion that Kenya is of concern, I'd like to bring the Lords' attention to more pressing matters at hand. Specifically the Irish problem."

It wasn't lost on most of the Lords that Loughty himself was an Irishman. He had however, lived most of his life in England and had lost all trace of his accent. But some suspected his loyalties remained with those living in Éire.

The Chamber remained quiet to give Loughty his opportunity to address the issue. It was well known that Ireland was indeed a sore and pressing concern for the British Government. With the founding of the Irish Republican Militia several years before, the relationship between Ireland and the United Kingdom had only become more difficult. This was coming to a head with the ongoing Irish War of Independence and the self proclaimed birth of the Irish Republic in 1919 under the Dáil.

"My Lords," continued Loughty, standing taller now, and thrusting his shoulders back, "I fear that calamity is nigh upon us if the Government will not come to talks with the representatives of the Irish Republic."

This met with boos, hisses and also polite applause, depending on which side of the throne you sat. The Opposition tending to the later and the Government tending to the former. Though Loughty was right. At least in Eric's estimation.

"Have we not learnt anything from the Great War that ended but just a whisper ago?" said Loughty. "And yet barely with its last dying gasp is born what I fear will become a new and ongoing war against our own people. Has war not taught us that dialogue is better than divisiveness?"

Loughty looked around as the crowd took turns jeering and applauding him. Eric smiled wistfully. If this was supposed to be the Upper House, if these were supposed to be the cream of England's crop, he worried about the very future of England and her empire. If educated, wealthy men could not communicate in a civilized fashion, perhaps the sun was just now setting on the empire that had reached the far corners of the globe. Perhaps the gods were no longer pleased.

"And what does the Lord propose?" came a sarcastic voice from the Government's Bench.

Eric didn't see who it was, but he had an idea. It didn't matter though. As much as he thought Loughty's argument was on point, it was unlikely that a coalition government in the current form under Lloyd George was about to do any negotiations with what it considered to be domestic terrorists.

Loughty looked over at the Government's Bench searching the faces of the Lords for the sarcastic speaker. He didn't find him. Not to worry, Loughty put on a charming smiled and nodded at them collectively.

"It is simply a matter of dialogue as I mentioned before. My proposal is to form a committee, either with us in the Upper House or even within the Members of Parliament. Whether it be the House of Lords or the House of Commons that forms such a committee is moot. The important thing is that such a committee is formed. For I fear that if we do not, we shall soon enough see blood in the streets. We shall spill English and Irish blood upon our own lands. And that, my Lords, would be a far greater tragedy than negotiating some sort of peace with our own people."

Loughty let the murmurs of the crowd swirl and pool in the Lords Chamber until it slowly emptied through the drain of time. He remained standing for a short while, marshaling his thoughts. Lord Paussage stood again. He looked over at the Lord Chancellor who nodded at him.

"If it please my Lords, I'd like to take my noble friend to task with his shameless love for the Emerald Isle."

Paussage smiled, though it was more a snarl really. His face was hard to like. Not only because he was a heavy drinker and an irascible man, but because his smiles always seemed to look sinister like a snarl. One could never be sure if he was being genuinely friendly or just getting ready to tear a piece from you. The Government's Bench erupted in raucous laughter and cheering. Loughty smiled though he held his shoulders back.

"It is no secret that I was born in Ireland. But it should also be apparent to any Lord with moderately good eyesight that I have served His Majesty and England for longer than my noble friend on the Government's Bench."

Now it was the Opposition's chance aided by the crossbenchers to rouse support for the lanky Lord. Paussage nodded slightly at Loughty. If he was irascible he still nevertheless took well to acerbic wit.

"And that is what worries my Lords. Are those Irish eyes smiling because my noble friend is genuinely interested in peace or is it the glimmer of wishing to further divide our nation?" asked Paussage rhetorically.

"I shall not stoop to such low character assassination as I have been the subject of. Those whose input on this matter is important know the answer to Lord Paussage's rhetoric. I only ask that we put forward a motion that the Government be force to the table to negotiate in good faith with the IRM. After all, has Dáil not been elected freely just like our own Government?" asked Loughty.

There was more raucousness in the Lords Chamber, and both Paussage and Loughty stood silently until it had swept itself away again.

"I believe my noble friend is choosing his facts far too loosely. The Irish people have not voted for independence. I am not aware of any referendum to that effect. Am I mistaken?" asked Paussage looking around at his fellow benchers.

There was a general agreement with his feeling. And indeed, to be fair, the Irish people had not yet held a referendum to remove themselves from the Government of the United Kingdom.

"There might not have been a referendum, but the people of Ireland have spoken loudly enough of their feelings. Just this past election they have sent seventy three members of Ceann Daoine to Parliament from the allotted one hundred and five. Is that not argument enough that they wish to form their own government?" asked Loughty.

Loughty was shouted down. The Chamber was becoming ever more antagonistic towards him as Eric thought they might. Though he feared that Loughty was right. There would be no good outcome if the Government refused to sit down and take their demands seriously. As far as he was concerned, if Ireland wanted to break away so be it. Let them. It was far better than fighting a civil war that could drag on for years.

"We cannot deal with terrorists," shouted Paussage who was by this time becoming visibly upset. "The Irish are a farming and tribal people. They cannot be relied upon to govern themselves civilly amongst a civilized nation. I say the Government and you, my Lords, should not vote to force the Government to sit down with these belligerents. Not until they have put down their weapons and beat their swords back into ploughs. No. We cannot allow for violence to steal us from our resolve. Or next we'll be dealing with the Scots looking to secede."

The Lords on the Government's side loved this. There was applause and cheering. Eric looked up at Loughty. His Irish eyes were no longer smiling. They were smoldering. And perhaps some years before, perhaps many years before, Loughty might have gone over to Paussage and punched him in the mouth for his rude remarks, and Eric would have cheered him on.

Today however, Loughty stood there, clenching his teeth. Resigned, as Eric was, that as a crossbencher, one would likely remain a groomsman and never the groom. At length the Lord Chancellor stood again and waited for a moment until all the hubris had been emptied from the minds of senile old men. Though that was not what he was thinking. Then he turned to Paussage and nodded. After that he turned to Loughty and smiled insincerely.

"If there is no one else who wishes to speak to this motion, do I have approval that the noble Lord be no longer heard?" said Marphallow.

Marphallow was awarded with general murmurs of agreement. He nodded his head. Loughty and Paussage remained standing.

"Good," said Marphallow. "Shall we then vote on Lord Loughty's motion?"

It was another rhetorical question. He was not waiting for an answer. Rather, he was waiting for his lungs to catch a breath.

"I'll now put the question to you, my Lords. Should our Government be forced to meet with representatives of the Irish Republican Militia or their quasi governmental leaders to discuss their wish to form their own government?"

Starting with the Government's Bench, the Lords voiced their content or discontent with the motion. By the time it came to Eric he knew what the outcome would be.

"Content," he said.

But he had heard more "not content" than he was expecting. Not that Loughty's motion had any real chance of being given a chance. And it would never have gotten past the House of Commons. But Eric nevertheless felt that the "content" votes that he could count perhaps on only both his hands were still too few.

CHAPTER TWO

Day Before Bloody Sunday

IT was raining lightly in Dublin on Saturday the twentieth of November, 1920. It was cold enough that the noses of people on the street were red, as were their cheeks. The complexions were ruddy and breath snaked around their necks like grey scarves. Dublin was a bustling town. The largest town in Ireland and the seat of government for the Irish Republic.

You couldn't see England from the docks that jutted up against the Irish Sea. But you could feel her presence. Prickly and pompous like the Brits that roamed the streets of Dublin as if it were their natural birthright. At least that's how Patrick Cooney felt. He had a seething dislike for the British Government. Nothing personal against Brits, but the Black and Tans and the soldiers. He'd sooner drive them out into the sea like St. Patrick did to the snakes.

Cooney was pacing up and down the boardwalk like an agitated panther, his black woolen coat with the collar turned up protecting him from the damp cold. He bit a cigarette between his lips. A hand rolled one and over his head a newsboy cap protected him from the light rain. It was early in the morning. He'd been up since before the sun. Not that you could see it, but you could tell it was there for the sky was a smear of light grey. Cooney was waiting for the others. They'd soon be here.

He finished his cigarette and stubbed it out under his shoe. He walked into the abandoned building. Dublin hadn't yet seen much economic improvement since the war ended, and half the docks were empty. It made it easier for him, and the IRM. Today was a big day. Tomorrow would be a bigger day if they'd just follow the plan. That was today's itinerary. Making sure everyone followed the plan.

The wooden building was as cold and damp inside as it was outside. The lights didn't work, but there was enough light brought in from outside to make it cozy. The big doors were open and the windows were plentiful if not high above the ground. That wasn't a bad thing necessarily. It allowed for some discretion.

Patrick Cooney pulled over a wooden crate and sat on it. He crossed his one leg over the knee of the other and waited. He was not a patient man, but he had learned patience in his long struggle against the English. Cooney was an unremarkable man to look at. Stocky of build with a round face and short stature. He reminded one of a bull dog. His hair was jet black and straight. His eyes were small but with a practiced piercing stare. His mouth was thin and closed unless he had something to say. He rarely smiled.

The first to arrive was Aidan Boyle. A thin slight man with a temper as quick as a firecracker. He had a red mess of hair and freckles across his face. He looked impish and his eyes twinkled and he smiled easily. Though he could turn on you in an instant.

"Aidan," said Cooney, nodding at him.

Aidan being five years senior to Cooney's thirty had introduced the younger man to the Irish Republican Fraternity. The IRF, some suggested, was the precursor to the IRM.

"Champion," said Aidan, smiling at Cooney.

Cooney got his nickname as a younger man in the boxing ring. It wasn't that he had been undefeated in the middleweight division of Ireland, but he'd only ever lost three matches. All by points. He could be knocked down, but he'd never been knocked out.

In ones and twos the rest of the men came slowly into the building. They huddled around Cooney as he waited. There would be eight of them all together. Including himself. Aidan Boyle was here. Cathal McClery had arrived. A tall man prematurely grey but with a full head of hair. Shortly after him Daire Nolan came in with Fintan O'Bern. The two of them could be brothers. Good looking men of average height with coal black wavy hair. Dark brown eyes. Jarlath Payne came in just minutes after Nolan and O'Bern. He was followed by an out of breath Nial Rowe. A chubby lad who looked younger than his age. He wasn't the toughest of them, but he was one of the most eager. They were waiting for Tadgh Ahearn.

He wasn't usually late. But this morning he was. After about five minutes, Cooney stood up.

"We may as well get started. None of you seen Tadgh?" he asked.

He was met with shrugs, upturned mouths and general blank stairs. Cooney furrowed his brow and looked down for a moment. He rubbed his chin with his hand.

"Well, let's get started then," he said. "We know where the men will be tomorrow. Are you all up for it?"

He looked around at the now somber faces. They nodded as his eyes met each of theirs. Motion came from the large door. They all turned to look. Tadhg Ahearn ran in and then took a moment to lean on his knees. He was out of breath. After a short while he looked up and grinned. Then he winced and gingerly touched the corner of his mouth with the back of his hand. He was bleeding from a small cut.

"Sorry I'm late lads," he said.

"Joseph and Mary," said Cooney, looking at him with a grim stare. "What the hell happened?"

Tadgh Ahearn was a tall man. Well over six feet and thin with it. He had a long thin face with bright blue eyes and a mess of curly brown hair. He was nice enough to look at but his teeth were all crooked. He grinned again at Cooney.

"Sorry, Champ," he said, "I had a bit of a chinwag with two of RIC's men."

His eyes were sparkling with delight. RIC was the Royal Irish Constabulary, and Tadgh was well known to them as were some of the others.

"And did they follow you here?" asked Cooney.

"No, I left them bellyaching a few blocks away. I left them down in Irishtown. They didn't follow me."

Cooney nodded.

"Good," he said. "What did they want?"

"The usual. They were asking about my business. Where I was going. That sort of thing."

"And did you tell them?"

Ahearn cocked his head in surprise.

"You really think I'd have told them that? I told them I'd just come home from meeting their mothers. They didn't like that too much."

"I imagine they didn't. I see they split your lip."

"More like a kiss compared to how I gave it back."

Cooney nodded.

"Good. We're glad you're well. Can we get back to it?"

Ahearn shrugged with his palms facing up. He huddled in around the group, standing taller than any of them. He patted the back of Rowe who looked up and grinned at him.

"Like I was saying," continued Cooney. "We all know

how it's going to be, right?"

He looked around at faces that nodded somberly. This wasn't going to be their biggest act but it was hopefully going to rattle the sabers to bring the English Government to the table. Cooney took a piece of chalk out of his pocket. It was white. He drew a map on the ground in front of his crate. It was a map of a neighborhood block. He pointed to the bottom left corner. Where two roads intersected.

"This here is Cavannagh Street," he said, dragging the chalk up and down the vertical street. "And this here is Soligmore Avenue." He dragged the chalk lengthwise along the horizontal street. "You all know it, right?"

He looked up from his map. More nodding faces. He looked back down and stabbed at what looked like a drawing of a house on that corner with a cross on the roof.

"The British Army think that they can find shelter in this church of theirs. This here is St. Thomas' Church. Church of the doubters."

The group around him laughed. That wasn't what it was really called. At least not the doubters part. Cooney looked up and let a small smile curl the corners of his mouth. But not for long.

"Now in the back on the right side," he said, drawing an arc from Soligmore Avenue up and around the right side of the church to the back of it on the far side of Cavannagh Street, "is an entrance way to the basement. It's there in the basement where they're going to be meeting tomorrow at nine, just before the ten o'clock service."

"And we're going to take them at nine fifteen right?" asked Ahearn.

Cooney looked up and nodded.

"Yeah. Nine fifteen sharp. We're gonna meet at The Long Limerick. You all know the pub?"

Cooney looked up and was met with nods.

"Nine in the morning we're gonna meet there. Nine sharp. And from there we'll make our way down here. Shouldn't take longer than fifteen minutes. Closer to ten."

Cooney looked up again. Dour faces. Only Ahearn was grinning.

"Any questions?" asked Cooney.

"Who's gonna be there?" asked Payne.

"My sources say there'll be fourteen men holed up there. Twelve are British Army, secret service agents, one of them will be Tadgh's beloved RIC, and the last one is a traitor. An informant."

"What are their names?" asked McClery.

Cooney looked up at him and frowned.

"Names aren't important. What is important is that these men all end up dead after we've finished. Look here, these are the founding members of the Istanbul Squad. Right? These are the men who we've been hunting for years now. They're the ones that are the biggest threat to our sovereignty. They know how to infiltrate and to interrogate Irish civilians. They are not nice men. And they'll be our downfall if we don't end this Squad. These fourteen. Well, the twelve British Army Officers specifically are key members of the Istanbul Squad. If we carry this off, the government will be more inclined to talk to us. I'm sure of it."

Cooney looked up at McClery. He frowned at him. He was trying to figure out why he was concerned about their names. Sounded like he might be a double agent. Cooney was going to have to keep an eye on him. McClery had never given him reason to be suspicious before, but this was an odd question.

"Alright," said Cooney. "You've all got your 1910s ready and fully loaded right?"

Cooney went around the group getting an affirmative from each of them in turn.

"It's a great gun," said Rowe, grinning. "Nice of you to get them for us."

"That's thanks to our lads at the dock," he said. "Now, Ahearn and I have the Browning rifles. We'll lead the attack and enter shooting as much as we can. We go in, and then the rest of you flank Ahearn and I. We fire until none of them are left standing. And then we make sure they're all dead. A bullet to the head if you need to make sure. Are we clear?"

They were all clear. These were not men who had just come together to express their dissatisfaction with the British Government. No. These were men who had been fighting since they were two bricks and a ticky high. They were used to violence, but more than that, they were patriotic and they believed they fought on the side of angels. They were freedom fighters or so they thought. And desperate times called for desperate measures.

CHAPTER THREE

New York Docks

IT was coming on five in the morning. Jersey City behind them was dark. The water in New York Harbor was black, oily and dark. It looked to have a thick, blubbery skin like a whale. It breathed slowly and regularly. Pieces of stars and the moon sparkled off its back like sprites. It was dark out here. On the pier of Port Jersey Brogan Quinn sucked on a hand rolled cigarette as he watched his men unloading cases from a container.

Quinn was one of The Blue Eyed Boys. His older brother and a couple of other lads had started the gang in the early 1900s. They'd all had blue eyes back then. Not all of his men had blue eyes now. But it wasn't a prerequisite. Loyalty and dedication were. It helped if you were tough too. Coghlan, his older brother had been dead a few years now, but that hadn't stopped Quinn from making The Blue- Eyed Boys the biggest Irish gang on the Eastern Seaboard.

Quinn was a slight man. He was in his early forties and wore a newsboy cap. He was five and a half feet in shoes with a creased face and a nose that God had stuck on haphazardly. But his eyes were bright and blue and he smiled easily. But the smile was sharp as a knife. He was generous to those who were loyal and ruthless to those who weren't.

He brought his watch up to his face and inhaled on his cigarette to give him some light by which to see the time. In front of him was the grey outline of the old lady. The Statue of Liberty. Her torch barely a glimmer of hope in the dark night. It was five minutes to five. Tommy Malone was meeting them at five. Quinn looked up and walked over to his right hand Anraí Dolan. Dolan was the opposite of Quinn. As small as Quinn was, Dolan was large. A towering impressive stocky hulk of a man. A good foot taller than Quinn with over a hundred and fifty pounds on him. He was, though, a friendly giant. Slow to anger, and reticent in the use of violence, he was both capable, loyal and willing when the need arose. He had brown hair and brown eyes. Not one of the founding members of The BlueEyed Boys.

"How you coming along, Anraí?" asked Quinn.

Dolan turned his impressive bulk towards his boss. He looked down at him and nodded.

"We're just about ready," he said.

Quinn looked round the big man into the container. It was almost empty. Eight cases were left. Five needed to be put into the back of the truck for Tommy Malone. Just as he was thinking about that, he heard the dull purring of an engine approaching. The lights of the car were showing first, but the car was concealed behind a container.

"Ready, lads," said Quinn, as he reached behind him and put his hand around his Colt 1911 in his waistband, "could be Malone, could not be."

He dropped the cigarette and squashed it out with his shoe. The car came around the corner. It was a black Cadillac. Quinn knew it as Malone's. As the car turned the corner and its lights swept over the legs of Quinn and his men, it came to a stop and the lights went out. Quinn started up to the car. He turned around, "hurry it up," he said to Dolan.

As he approached the Cadillac, Malone got out of the passenger side. Two of his men got out the back. They were heavily armed. His driver stayed behind the wheel.

Malone was just a few inches taller than Quinn, which wasn't hard to do. Though he had about fifty pounds on him. Malone had been the boss of the West Side Crew for over ten years. The largest Italian Mafia group on the Eastern Seaboard. They were bigger than The Blue-Eyed Boys and getting bigger by the minute. Malone had a head for business. He was expanding into Chicago and then west from there. Malone took the cigar that barely burned out of his mouth and clutched it between chubby fingers with rings on most fingers.

"The whisky came in good?" he asked Quinn.

Quinn nodded.

"Not a drop spilled. Fifty cases like we agreed. Red Beagle Whisky. Ireland's finest."

Dolan came up to Quinn and leaned down to whisper into his ear.

"All done, boss," he said.

Quinn nodded, still facing Malone.

"My lads have just finished up. Why don't you come and have a look," said Quinn, and then he looked at Dolan, "open up a bottle of ours for Malone to sample."

Dolan nodded and hulked off towards the container. Quinn led Malone towards the truck which was off to the left side of the container. It was filled with cases of Irish whisky. Malone walked around the back of the truck, looking at the cases. They were all stamped with the logo and name of the whisky. The logo had a beagle standing at the ready. Underneath it was the name "Red Beagle Whisky".

Dolan came along with a couple of tumblers and a bottle of unopened whisky. He handed the bottle to Quinn and held the tumblers. Quinn opened the bottle and poured a finger in each glass. Dolan passed one to Malone and Quinn took the other.

Always a cautious man, Malone waited until Quinn had taken a sip first before trying it himself. It was strong, smoky and good. Malone raised his glass up to

Quinn who mirrored him.

"You Irish sure know how to make a good whisky. Better than the Scottish."

Malone was nothing if he wasn't charming. But he was speaking the truth. He did prefer Irish whisky to Scottish. Besides, it was easier getting Irish whisky with his connection Quinn, especially under the newly enacted prohibition. A rare opportunity for profit that the government had just offered him on a silver platter.

"Sláinte," said Quinn.

"Salute," replied Malone.

Malone finished the rest with one swallow. Quinn did the same. Malone looked behind him and then motioned with his right hand. The hand that still had a cigar in it. One of the passengers who had not stayed by Malone's side opened up the trunk and took out a suitcase. He brought that up to Malone and handed it to him. Malone handed it over to Quinn.

"Here's the money. Fifty cases of twelve bottles a case. Sixty thousand dollars for your whisky."

Malone smiled at Quinn like he was a benevolent benefactor. Quinn handed the case to Dolan who opened it and lay it on the side of the truck to count.

"As promised," said Quinn. "It's good doing business with you."

Malone nodded.

"You said you could get more of this whisky," said Malone.

Quinn nodded.

"I'm going to need a lot more."

"How much?"

"This much on a weekly basis."

Quinn stared at Malone steadily. He wasn't sure he wanted to get into that much business with the Italian. But sixty thousand dollars a week would sure help him expand. He'd have to pay up front to his contact in Ireland. But it was manageable. At length Quinn nodded.

"I can do that," he said. "But I'll have to miss a week in order to set it up. Fifty cases a week? You sure?"

Malone nodded, still grinning.

"I'll need half up front for good faith and to take care of the inspectors and the people on the other end."

Malone nodded slowly.

"It's in there already."

Malone looked past Quinn to the suitcase that Dolan was just finishing up counting. Quinn looked behind at Dolan. Dolan closed the suitcase and nodded.

"Ninety thousand like he promised," said Dolan to Quinn.

Quinn looked back at the Italian.

"I'm a man of my word when it comes to business," he said, then in a more somber tone. "You will be too."

Quinn looked at him and nodded.

"Always am."

They shook hands and the heavily armed man standing next to Malone walked off towards the truck. He secured the cargo under a tarpaulin cover and climbed into the driver's seat. Malone walked back towards his Cadillac with the other heavily armed man walking back with him. Quinn watched Malone get into the back seat as his armed man got into the passenger side across from the driver. The truck started and then slowly rolled away. The Cadillac came to life and the lights blinded Quinn momentarily until they swept away. Malone waved casually at Quinn as they drove by. His cigar stuck firmly in his mouth. Quinn nodded.

Dolan walked up to him and they watched the Italians drive away slowly until they were gone and there was no sight nor sound of them left. Quinn stared after them for a long while.

"Think it's a good idea doing business with them, boss?" asked Dolan.

Quinn didn't look at him. He stared straight ahead as if trying to see the future.

"It's a good idea for now," he said. Then he turned around and started walking back towards the almost empty container.

"Let's get the rest of the whisky into our cars and head on out of here before trouble starts coming to look for us. We've got some celebrating to do."

CHAPTER FOUR

Marmalade Park

THERE was a light rain falling in London on Monday when Lady Marmalade came down for breakfast. It was the day after Bloody Sunday. The twenty second of November. Eric was sitting at the table reading the paper. There were no plates in front of him. Either he had eaten already or he was waiting for Frances. He tucked the paper over itself as Frances came over to him and kissed him on the lips.

"Good morning, darling," she said.

"Morning, my love," he replied.

"Have you eaten?" she asked.

"No, I wasn't too hungry so I thought I'd wait for you."

Frances smiled at him and took a seat to his left. She could see out into the garden. It was a grey day. Thick with mist and fog and the window pane was dotted with small droplets of rain. The grass was green but there weren't many flowers out in the garden.

"Thank you for waiting, darling. What are we having?"

Eric folded up the newspaper once more and put it to his right. Lady Marmalade could see part of the headline. Irish violence, or something like that, is what it said.

"I've had Ginny cook up our regular. Bacon and eggs. Some toast. Anything else you might like?"

"Sounds lovely."

Alfred came up to her right.

"Tea for my Lady?" he asked.

Frances looked up at him, nodded and smiled.

"Sounds lovely, Alfred," she said. "Looks like a creamy tea sort of day."

"Quite right," he said, as he poured the rusty liquid into a teacup. After he was done, he moved away. Out of sight, but not out of reach. Frances poured some cream into her tea and added a sugar. She stirred it absentmindedly. Tea etiquette had never held much interest for her. Milk before the tea, or after, made no difference from what she could tell. But the cream, yes, that was the key.

"I assume Declan and Amelia got off to school without a problem this morning?" Frances asked Eric.

"Yes, Alfred just got back from dropping them off not too long ago. Declan seemed a little worried, he has an English exam today. Amelia was in good spirits."

Frances smiled. Declan was a studious young boy, if not a bit too serious. Though he did have the marks to show for it.

"Are you off to work today or to parliament?" asked Frances.

Eric leaned onto the table and shook his head.

"I think I'll be off to work. I don't think I can stomach much more posturing from the Lords this morning. Have you seen the news?"

Frances shook her head.

"No, obviously not good though. Irish problems again?"

"That's putting it lightly. They've murdered fourteen men. Twelve British Army members, an informant and a member of the Royal Irish Constabulary."

Eric leaned back as Ginny came in carrying a large silver tray of the food. Frances caught a whiff of the bacon and eggs before she saw her. Ginny placed the tray on a dumb waiter and then served them up. She put a plate with four rashers of bacon and one fried egg in front of Lady Marmalade, then she put a plate with six rashers of bacon and two fried eggs in front of Lord Marmalade. Then she placed a rack of toast with four pieces between them along with the butter and marmalade.

"Thank you, Ginny," said Frances, smiling and looking at her.

Ginny smiled back, bowed and went back to the

kitchen to her duties and chores. Frances sipped her tea and hummed.

"Smells delicious," she said. "I didn't realize how famished I was."

"You can always have her cook up some more if you'd like."

"I don't think it'll be necessary," she said. "Not with the toast as well."

Eric and Frances went to eating their food for a while in silence. Frances sipped her tea and looked out the window at the grey day.

"What are the Irish up to do you think, darling?" she asked.

Eric looked up from his plate. He put his fork and knife down and shook his head wearily.

"I know exactly what they're up to. They want independence from the crown. Thing is, it's not going to happen. Not if they carry on like they are. I'm certain there'll be a huge and excessive response in the coming days."

Frances shook her head. She found the whole thing quite tragic.

"Are you sure?"

Eric nodded slowly and sadly.

"It came up in Parliament," he said. "Lord Loughty wanted to bring a motion forward which wasn't ever going to happen and so they killed it."

"What did he want?"

"He wanted a motion passed that required the

government to set up a commission or committee to meet with the IRM and Ceann Daoine. Nothing radical really. But you know how the Lords can get. Stick in the muds the bunch of them."

"And I suppose that Loughty's background being Irish didn't endear him to anyone either," said Frances, smiling and then sipping at her tea.

Eric nodded and smiled at her.

"Of course not. I think some of them, Lord Paussage in particular, did it almost out of spite."

"I never did like him. Quite the temper, a big drinker and all round unpleasant pompous sod."

Eric laughed out loud and slapped the table.

"You're quite right, and quite honest too."

Frances smiled and ate some egg.

"I could tell Loughty was upset by the whole thing. But he put on a brave face. You know, my love, I sometimes wonder why I ever even attend these sorts of things. If it wasn't for the Commons I fear England would be driven off a cliff if just out of the sheer incompetence of these entitled men."

Eric put his head down and studied his food for a moment. Then he went to eating once again. He put a piece of bacon on his fork and then pierced on a piece of egg.

"I for one, just don't understand," said Frances, "why our government is so bent on war when we just narrowly won the last one. Do lessons never get learnt?"

Eric looked up at her. He reached for the salt shaker and shook more salt on his eggs and bacon. He reached for the pepper grinder and did the same.

"It appears we have incompetent nincompoops running the show," he said without any sign of irony. "And they're intent to drive us into debt, destitution or death. Perhaps all three."

Frances nodded and put more egg into her mouth. She chewed carefully and slowly as if in rhythm to her thoughts.

"I don't see the harm in at least talking with them. If it were to save just one life it would be worth it. In fact, if truth be told, I don't know why we don't just meet with them and hammer out their secession."

"I agree," said Eric, "though I think I understand why men don't want to."

"Why?"

"Egos primarily, and concern that this might start a cascade of Scotland and Wales looking for the same."

Frances furrowed her eyebrows.

"I can't really see that happening," she said. "Scotland and Wales have been part of the kingdom for hundreds of years. Over three hundred for Scotland and almost five hundred for Wales if I remember my history lessons."

"I'll take your word for it, my love, and I think you're right. I don't see any independence movement in either of those countries. I'm just offering what I think are some of the political reasons for those in government not wanting to sit down with the IRM."

"Or perhaps it could be pure apathy," said Frances with a sparkle in her eye.

Eric laughed again and drank some tea. He looked over at Alfred standing quietly and stoically off to the side against the wall.

"I think we should ask our resident Irishman," he said.

Frances shook her head.

"I don't think Alfred wants to get involved in our discussion."

"Well, I for one am curious on his insights," said Eric. "What do you think, Alfred?"

Alfred came forward and smiled at Eric.

"Of what my Lord?"

"Of this Irish War of Independence."

"I try to stay out of politics, my Lord, a dirty business, if you'll pardon me for saying so," said Alfred.

Alfred was just a year older than Lady Marmalade, though he had been in England for almost as long as he had been in Ireland.

"I agree wholeheartedly. It is a dirty business, though not as dirty as war, don't you agree?" asked Eric.

Alfred nodded.

"Yes, sir," he said.

"Go on then," said Eric, "give us your thoughts."

"Well to be honest, my Lord, I consider England to

be my home. I've been here almost as long as I was born and raised in Ireland." Alfred paused for a moment. "If I could be quite honest."

Eric nodded.

"I expect nothing less."

"Well, sir, I find war abhorrent. Nothing good comes of it, as we've seen from the Great one we just had. Even though we won it, I wouldn't say it improved things much for most of us."

"I quite agree," said Eric.

"I fear, my Lord, that the same outcome will come of the IRM's War of Independence. I understand the Irish people are a proud people. We're proud of our land, but I think that joining with the rest of the United Kingdom would do us more favors than it would hurt."

"That's a reasoned decision, Alfred. I wish half the Lords had as much common sense as you do."

"I don't disagree with Alfred," said Frances, looking at her husband, "but that's not really our decision to make. If the Irish want to determine their own future as part of the United Kingdom or not, then we ought to honor that."

Eric ate more of his eggs and bacon. Then he sipped on the tea.

"I agree. Fourteen lives lost in yesterday's attack. Both British and Irish. For what? Not much that I can see. I agree with you, my love, that we should let the Irish have a referendum on the idea. Though I wonder if we did, and it didn't pass that these terrorists might still continue the fight for freedom. The stubbornness of the zealot if you will."

"Quite possibly, darling, but isn't that a risk we take for living in a democracy?"

Frances spread butter and then marmalade on a slice of toast. She took a bite of it. Eric put the last forkful of eggs and bacon in his mouth. As he chewed, he buttered his toast and then slathered large chunks of the marmalade on top.

"Yes, you're right," he said. "These are just some of the fears of the Lords who are antagonistic towards this idea."

"Well, I suppose they'll have to get over it. Another reason why the House of Lords should be elected and not merely appointed," said Frances.

Eric looked up at her and smiled.

"I'd never get in," he said, grinning at her.

"Nonsense," said Frances, holding her toast in front of her as she used it to gesture as she spoke. "I'm sure you'd get in. In fact, I know I'd certainly vote for you."

Frances took another bite of toast.

"How kind," said Eric, grinning sarcastically, "I'm comforted by your largesse."

Frances frowned at him.

"You really would get elected, I'm sure of it," she said.

"Yes, perhaps you're right. However, I don't see that happening anytime soon. There is a long and rich history of Lords being appointed, and I don't see the powers that be changing that anytime soon."

"Three hundred odd years does not a history make," said Frances. "It is merely a convenience, and an ill conceived one at that. But then again, I suppose one should never hope for the King to abdicate voluntarily. So too would the Lords never want to go quietly into becoming accountable. Heaven forbid."

"Heaven forbid indeed," said Eric. "The government might actually get some things done. Your gentle opinions are one of the things that I love about you. You are a forceful woman."

"Only because I voice my mind. Pity the women that remain as timid as kept pets. No wonder we haven't yet won suffrage."

Eric looked up and sighed.

"The right to vote is not the great equalizer that some might think."

"Of course not, darling, but it would be a start. Unless we're treated equally as men by all levels of government, we'll never undo sexism and misogyny."

"I know," said Eric, biting at his toast. "It's coming. The movements are forming and strengthening. Already women have won the vote at the local level for some time. And you've had the chance to vote for two years now."

"Thanks to my age and position of wealth," she said.

Eric nodded.

"Still, it is a start. And amongst the peers there is

growing, albeit begrudging, support."

"How comforting," said Frances.

Eric laughed aloud. Frances put the last piece of toast in her mouth.

"You are a rapscallion," said Eric.

They sat in silence for a while. Drinking tea while Frances slowly finished her meal.

"Back to our original conversation," she said. "What do you think the real chances are of averting more tragedies over the Irish issue?"

Eric looked up at her.

"Not good, my love," he said. "They won't talk, and I fear that without dialogue, men will resort to the blunt instrument of violence."

Frances smiled insincerely. It was as she had feared. Outside the rain still came down. Slow and steady, like the shuffling of old men. It was a day marked by sadness, and the weather was adamant to remind you of such. Frances buttered another slice of toast and put marmalade on it. She poured herself more tea. Added more cream and sugar and stirred it absentmindedly. She continued to look outside.

"You think that the government will move forcefully against the IRM on this recent attack?" she asked Eric, not looking at him.

"I'm certain of it," said Eric, leaning back, cradling his teacup and saucer in front of him, looking at his wife quizzically.

"Then I am certain that the Irish problem as some

would like to call it, will become an English problem soon enough."

"What do you mean?" asked Eric.

Frances looked over at her husband. She took the spoon out of her tea and placed it on the saucer.

"Well, so far, the IRM has not been very antagonistic towards England. All of these attacks have taken place on Irish soil. If England goes into Ireland, and as we are wont to do, with too heavy a hand, I can foresee the Irish coming over to England to make their voices heard more loudly."

"You mean to suggest that the next attack might actually be on English soil?"

Frances looked at her husband and turned her mouth down. She nodded sadly.

"That is exactly what I fear," she said.

Eric looked at Lady Marmalade steadily for a while, over the rim of his teacup. He took a slow sip. The tea was barely lukewarm.

"I will try and suggest that outcome to the Lords," said Eric. Though quietly in his mind he knew that would likely be a difficulty he wasn't sure he had the stamina for.

"I can't say for certain," said Lady Marmalade, "but that would be my suspicion. Though as you know, my dear, I'd love to be wrong. In fact, I desperately hope that I'm wrong."

Frances sipped her tea over the barely audible tapping of the rain agains the windowpane. She wondered if the rain was going to continue throughout the day or if sunny skies might come out later. If her mind was any indication, she felt the latter was likely out of the question.

"I hope you're wrong too, my love," said Eric. "Though I've always given your opinions heavy weighting, for you are not often wrong."

He smiled ruefully.

"Perhaps I should attend the House of Lords after all," he added.

Frances looked over at him and smiled.

"You could always speak to Baron Marphallow tonight. Perhaps calling on him at home might be a better approach. You have a way with persuading others when you're in a more intimate setting."

Eric nodded.

"Yes, I think that will be a better idea."

Eric drained his tea and sat the cup and saucer back on the table. He stood up and came over to Lady Marmalade's side. He bent down and kissed her on the cheek.

"I'll be off then," he said. "Don't get up my love, I'll see myself out."

"Have a good day, my darling," said Frances.

He nodded and smiled at her and turned to face Alfred.

"I'll drive myself in today," he said. "Make sure Frances doesn't get into any trouble if you can help it."

"I will do my best, my Lord."

Eric nodded, smiling at Alfred. He patted him on the shoulder.

"You're a good man," he said, and with that he walked out of the room.

Frances took a bite of her second slice of toast. It was cold and she realized she wasn't that hungry anymore. She put it down and picked up her teacup. She sipped her tea and stared out of the window. After a time, she reached over for Eric's newspaper and opened it up to read about the ongoing problems the Irish were having. She eagerly hoped her feelings and intuition were wrong about the problems spilling over onto England.

CHAPTER FIVE

The Bishops Avenue

THE three men were sitting in Baron Marphallow's smoking room. Marphallow was smoking on a large cigar. It suited him. For he was a large and rotund man with a ruddy hue that was only outshone by the lit end of his cigar. Lord Paussage was there too. He was standing with a cigarette in one hand and a tumbler of whisky in the other. Lord Loughty was standing with his back to both men. His tumbler of whisky was on the table in front of him. The whisky told him everything he needed to know.

It was not Irish whisky. It was Scottish. And Marphallow had reminded him of that at least twice when it had been handed over. Paussage smirked at that. And Loughty's Irish eyes were no longer smiling.

He had been invited here, by Marphallow. Under what was now seen as a pretense. It had seemed that Marphallow had wanted to have an earnest and probing conversation with him over the Irish problem as everyone was calling it. Of course, no one had listened to him originally when he had voiced his concerns, and debate in the House had taken a decidedly acerbic tone towards the Irish. Loughty had thought Marphallow wanted to engage in reasoned conversation this evening. Away from the tempers and the outbursts. Only it wasn't to be.

Loughty picked up his tumbler and turned to face the other two men. Paussage was looking down at Marphallow who sat like a wet slug on a large couch. His face was damp with sweat. Marphallow brought the whisky to his lips and drank from it as if it were cooled tea. He made a scene of smacking his lips.

"Good Scottish whisky isn't it, Loughty?" he said, looking at the Irishman earnestly.

Loughty looked at Marphallow for a while trying to determine if the man was trying to stoke his Irish temper or if Marphallow was just ignorant. He chose to believe the latter.

"For a Scotsman's tea it's not bad," said Loughty with a straight face.

Marphallow laughed and slapped his thigh, ash falling on the couch like the dry leaves from a dead tree.

"You Irish sure do have a temper," said Marphallow.

"Aye, that's the truth," said Paussage with a Scottish accent. Though he was a Scotsmen his accent was not thick unless he liked it to be. Loughty raised his glass at Paussage.

"You make this tea then?" he asked.

The Scotsman had no retort, but his skin flushed hot and red as the lit end of his own cigarette. He puffed on it looking through the smoke at Loughty with eyes as hard and dead as grey marbles. Loughty met his stare over the rim of his own tumbler. If truth be told he'd be hard pressed to determine the origin of a whisky just by taste. Others might. But they'd be the ones with big red bulbous noses. Perhaps like Paussage, he thought.

"You Irish don't know how to make a proper whisky," said Paussage after some time. "It's the Scots that invented it."

"Not actually true," said Loughty, "the Irish invented whisky. But if it helps you to sleep at night, believe what you will."

"I'll wager you a hundred bob," said Paussage.

Loughty smiled at him.

"I thought you were a Lord," he said. "Let's talk real money. How about fifty pounds? One thousand bob."

"I'd make it ten thousand bob just to see the look on your face," said Paussage.

"The look on my face will be no different. I take no pleasure in taking money from fools."

Loughty smiled at Paussage and offered him his hand to shake. Paussage put his cigarette in his mouth and shook Loughty's hand. It was a hard squeeze, but not hard enough to be threatening.

"If you two gamblers have finished having your fun,

I did actually bring you both here to discuss the Irish problem."

The two of them broke off their handshake and stood facing Marphallow.

"I told you last week that there'd be problems," said Loughty.

"Yes," answered Marphallow, "and nobody likes a braggart."

"Incidentally," he continued, "a week isn't much time to prepare based on your thoughts and feelings at the time."

Loughty didn't answer that.

"You know how I feel," said Paussage.

Marphallow nodded.

"You feel the same as most of us on the government's side. But we must listen to all voices. Must we not?"

It was a rhetorical question, but Paussage felt obliged to answer it.

"I don't see why we must."

Paussage was beginning to get under Loughty's skin. He didn't like the man. He hated his arrogance and his high opinion of himself. He didn't feel much differently towards Marphallow. The fat wet frog that sat squat in front of him.

"Yes, well, I think we should listen to Loughty. He does have good ideas sometimes," said Marphallow.

"He's just going to tell us the very same thing he told us last time," said Paussage.

"Can I speak for myself?" interjected Loughty.

Paussage went over to the whisky bottle which was on a table behind Marphallow. It was a light rusty brown color, not dissimilar to the whisky.

"Please go ahead," said Marphallow.

Loughty looked down at his tumbler which had less whisky in it than you'd need to drown a fly.

"Fact is, the IRM is using these tactics because they don't believe they're being heard. If they felt they were being heard, I rather doubt they'd be up to this sort of business."

Paussage returned with a half full tumbler of whisky. Marphallow was nursing his, likely because he'd had a couple before Loughty and Paussage had arrived.

"Do you speak for the IRM because you know them or because you're a part of them?" asked Paussage.

Paussage was getting courageous under the influence of the whisky. He was becoming more unlikeable with each passing minute and Loughty was worried what he might do if he overstayed his welcome, which was pretty much up.

"I am a watcher of human interactions. It is plain as day if you had any common sense that a reasonable man does not resort to violence if his grievances are being aired."

"You ask the government to put itself in a difficult position," said Marphallow, trying to break apart the two sparring partners. "If we start to negotiate with terrorists will it not just create an ugly precedent for others with grievances to start off violently rather than peacefully?"

"I don't think that will be much of a problem. Not if this issue is handled sensitively and quickly."

"I don't agree," said Paussage. "Treating violent men with pacifism is just asking for England to be treated as a door mat. We will have all sorts of disenfranchised banging down our doors in no time. We will be at war with all sorts of factions if we don't quell this Irish nonsense right away."

"It is not Irish nonsense," said Loughty, raising his voice. "The Irish have elected many members from Ceann Daoine to Parliament. They are requesting a voice in their own governance."

"Yes, indeed," shouted Paussage back, "the very same Ceann Daoine that is the puppet of the IRM. Ha!"

Paussage tossed his head back in contempt.

"Ceann Daoine has distanced themselves from the IRM," said Loughty, "everyone knows that."

"That may well be the case," said Marphallow, "but that is political talk. Nobody here can take them seriously at their word. Even you Loughty, can see through that if you're honest with yourself."

Loughty lowered his head and then drained the rest of his whisky. There was no drowned fly in it. Though he would have liked to have drowned Paussage.

"Very well," Loughty said at last. "I'll grant you that. But that does not mean that more reasonable heads won't prevail if we meet them halfway."

"Now you're admitting that Ceann Daoine is indeed just a political front for the IRM and you want us to believe that sitting down with terrorists is the solution to our problems," said Paussage. "I will not grant you that. The way you deal with any terrorist is the way you deal with bullies generally. You hit them hard and you hit them where it hurts."

"And where exactly is that?" asked Loughty, "they live and work amongst the Irish people."

"I believe His Majesty's Government has means to ferret the rats from their hoary dens. And if not, I can't say I'd shed a tear if we just razed the whole island," said Paussage.

Loughty looked at him. He was hot. He squeezed his empty tumbler just a little too hard.

"What did you say?" he asked.

They were interrupted by a woman entering the smoking room. She was rather plain. A dusty blond with her hair put up in a bun. She wore light makeup and a long dress. What she lacked in natural beauty she made up in a curvy figure. Her name was Agnes and she was Marphallow's wife. She was in her late twenties. Much younger than Marphallow. She had married him for money. That was as plain as the rain in Spain.

Agnes came up to Marphallow and kissed him on the cheek.

"I'm off to bed, Chris," she said, trying to cajole a

stingy warmth out of her voice.

She looked over at Paussage and smiled curtly, though her look lingered longer than it needed to. She broke eye contact from him and briefly looked at Loughty before returning her gaze to her husband.

"Alright, dear," said Marphallow. "Good night."

She smiled at him and looked over at Paussage who nodded at her. Then she looked at Loughty.

"Good night," he said, as he smiled.

Agnes turned around and walked out of the room. The men were silent until she had left. Paussage was the first to break the silence.

"You are a lucky man," he said to Marphallow, though he looked at the now closed door and sipped his whisky.

"Indeed," said Marphallow.

Silence strolled around the room like a cold breeze. Loughty turned and put his tumbler on the table opposite Marphallow. He'd had enough of the Scotsman's tea, and he didn't need to push his temper any further with what might come of another drink. He turned back around. He breathed deeply and tried his best to put his best face forward. There was no harm at this stage in pleading, if it would help salvage some peace from these difficult times.

"Creating a martyr of one, or of many for that matter, will only encourage greater unhappiness with England and the crown. You don't win friends by rubbing their noses in the dirt," said Loughty.

Paussage took a sip of his whisky.

"We're not trying to win friends," said Paussage, "we're just trying to keep peace in the country."

Loughty looked at him but didn't say anything.

"Listen, Larmer," said Marphallow, trying to comfort the tall man with his first name, "I don't see how we can allow such atrocities to go unpunished. Listen, I'm all for dialogue and negotiation, but the IRM and their foot soldiers need to put an end to the terrorism first. I just don't see another way."

Loughty shook his head.

"Look at it this way. Pretend that the IRM is a younger sibling. It's up to the older one to act more like the adult. England needs to make the first move to hearing them out. That's all they want. They just want to be heard."

"Yes, and to break free from our United Kingdom," said Paussage.

"And what's wrong with that?" asked Loughty.

"What's wrong with that is that we have English men and women living in Ireland who would not vote for it. And we have Irish men and women living in Ireland who would not vote for it, and we must protect them from the uninformed masses who would bring Ireland to her knees."

"And I suppose you know what's best for Ireland?" asked Loughty.

Paussage smirked at him.

"The Government knows what's better for Ireland,"

said Paussage.

"You pompous bastard," said Loughty, before collecting himself.

Marphallow raised his hand that held his cigar. The ash was growing long on it.

"Gentlemen," he said as if he were scolding schoolchildren, "this sort of language isn't going to get us anywhere. Your anger will get the better of you, Loughty, if you allow it. It is the one thing does not endear me to the Irish."

Loughty closed his eyes and clenched his jaw in frustration.

"Paussage here is just trying to goad me. And has it ever occurred to any of you that the Irish have a temper because they've been bullied by the English for so long."

"A savage, uncultured people do not understand anything that is not accompanied by the bite of the whip," said Paussage. "You thick micks don't want to help yourselves so we have to do it for you."

Loughty walked up to Paussage. It was a quick five steps. Before he knew what had hit him, Loughty's fist had smacked him right on the nose. Paussage stumbled backwards, his arms flailing and his tumbler tumbling through the air spilling whisky like an incontinent man's dribbles, before smashing to pieces on the floor.

"You ever call me a mick again and I'll smack you back into last year, you limey arse," spat Loughty.

He turned to leave but before he did, he looked at Marphallow.

"You brought me here under false pretenses. You have no desire to sit down with Ceann Daoine. It will be the death of you. I swear, this is just the beginning of what you think the Irish problem is."

Loughty spun around and stormed out of the house, grabbing his coat and slamming the door after himself before the butler had a chance to do it for him.

Marphallow sat, squat as ever, smoking his cigar and looking through the space that Loughty had just recently stood in. On his right, Paussage cursed the whole of Ireland and the Irish people. He clutched a white handkerchief to his bleeding nose.

"This is why we cannot sit down with those bastards," he said.

Marphallow nodded, still not looking at him.

"I quite agree," he said, blowing smoke from his mouth.

CHAPTER SIX

Kilburn London

THERE'S an old pub in Kilburn, London. It's called The Loyal Beagle. Some say it's the first Irish pub on English soil. What's not in disagreement is how long it's been there. It's been in the same location since 1579. It's a plain looking house with a red tiled roof. The roof used to be thatch. But thatch has a tendency to catch fire and it did in early September of 1666, but it had nothing to do with the Great Fire that engulfed London at the time. A disgruntled Englishman having had one too many and being kicked out tossed a lit rag soaked in oil onto the roof. And that is how The Loyal Beagle lost its first thatch roof.

More importantly related to our story is the fact that The Loyal Beagle is an Irish pub. An Irish pub on English soil during a time of tension. It had been built back in 1579 by the owner of Red Beagle Whisky which at the time was called Red Beagle Irish Whisky. Already during the sixteenth century, the Scots were trying to make a name for themselves as whisky producers and connoisseurs. And they were making good headway. The Irish had in fact rested on their laurels, comfortable in the knowledge that they were the first to have produced this heavenly elixir. But Jarlath Sheenan had a different idea. He wanted to expand his business. Give the Scots a run for their money with what was arguably the best whisky in the world at the time, Red Beagle Irish Whisky.

But all that history is of little relevance. On the evening of 22 November 1920 The Loyal Beagle pub was busy. And it wasn't just whisky that was on the menu. In a dark corner of the pub around a well worn and gnarled table that might have been as old as the building itself, sat four men. They were Irishmen. And it wasn't just the half empty bottle of Red Beagle Whisky that sat in the middle of the table. No, it was their accents and their conversation.

Lorcan Sheenan took a sip of the whisky in his tumbler and licked his lips. He was a fat man. Well fed with thick curly grey hair that ended in mutton chops around his jowls. He was in his early fifties. He was dressed well. You could tell he had money. He was a direct descendant of Jarlath and the current proprietor of The Loyal Beagle. Though you wouldn't know it for he was seldom here. He had come down however, for a pressing matter. He spent most of his time in Dublin where the Red Beagle distillery was.

"You can't just walk on into Bishops Avenue," said

Sheenan, "and not expect to be noticed."

A thin, gangly man looked at Sheenan and held his tumbler steady on the table.

"Well, we can't let Lord Marphallow squeeze us dry as we try to do business with Quinn and his lads," he said.

"That's not what I'm suggesting Niall," said Sheenan.

Niall Braden was Lorcan's right hand man and most trusted confident. He was in his seventies and had served with Lorcan's father. Nobody could be more trusted than Niall.

The other two men at the table looked at each other and sipped their whisky quietly. They hadn't said much. They were dressed a little rougher than the other two. Rumor had it that they served with the IRM. They had an intimate friendship with violence which was written in plain language across both their faces.

"Perhaps we can see what Oran and Padraig have to say on the matter," offered Niall.

Lorcan clenched his lips together and nodded slowly. He took another sip of his whisky and then looked over at the man to his left. This was Oran.

"You're familiar with these sorts of delicate matters. What do you suggest."

"My recommendation would be to get rid of the problem," he said plainly.

Lorcan squinted.

"What do you mean by get rid of the problem?"

"Exactly like I says. Make it permanent. This chap here doesn't listen to you, so you've got to get rid of him. Plain and simple."

"Oran, you're talking about a Baron here. There will be questions asked. You can't just make a man like that disappear."

Oran smiled at Lorcan.

"Sure you can. Done it before. And it makes no difference to me if he was the King of England. Just the same."

Lorcan looked over at Niall. Niall put his hand on Oran's forearm. Oran looked at the hand distastefully. Niall removed it. Oran took another long sip of whisky and helped himself to more.

"There must be other ways to impress upon the Baron the urgency of our needs," said Niall.

Oran looked over at his friend who still hadn't said much. Padraig nodded at him.

"There might be," he said. "This Baron of yours, he's married right? Got children then?"

Niall took a turn to squint as Oran was looking at him. Niall nodded slowly, unsurely.

"He's married, yes. But he doesn't have any children."

"That makes it easier. Him not having children. Still the best method is to have him disappear."

"But we don't want that," said Niall.

"Then you let us talk to the wife," said Oran.

Niall shook his head and squinted some more.

"But it's got nothing to do with her."

"It's always got something to do with her. You're just not hearing me clear. The way me and Padraig talk to her be a little different to how you might talk to her."

"You're suggesting that you make his wife disappear?" asked Niall, with incredulity in his voice.

"No, that wouldn't be right. She hadn't done nothing wrong. No sir, we just bruise the flower a little. That'll make your Baron reconsider your offer."

Lorcan shook his head. Niall looked down.

"No, I'm afraid that's even more unacceptable than the first option. You must have a third possibility. Niall promised me that you two were comfortable with fixing these sorts of problems. Besides it's better to have him alive for our future business purposes."

Oran looked back at Padraig and then he sipped on his whisky.

"Well, I suppose there is a third option. Though it'll cost you more for there be more difficulties in it."

"I'm listening," said Lorcan.

"My brother and me go and speak to this Baron of yours. We rough him a little. But like I said, we take more risk that way. A man like him might bring the full force of the law up against us. And there's one other little thing."

"What's that?" asked Lorcan.

"My brother sometimes gets a little carried away.

He takes a lot of pride in his work."

Lorcan sighed and looked at Niall.

"And how much do you want for this option?" Lorcan asked.

"That'll cost you five thousand quid. Two more than the first option. But like I says, it's only because there'll be more heat at our feet. If you want my opinion I'd recommend you does the first option and save yourself two thousand quid."

"I don't care much for any of the options frankly," said Lorcan.

"I can understand that," said Oran. "Life's simple if you just stick to the straight path. But that isn't what you've done is it?"

Lorcan gave Oran a stern look, but it had no bite to back it up. Oran had tangled with tougher men. Tougher of tongue and of leather. Oran finished up his whisky, and was about to pour himself another. Lorcan grabbed the bottle and brought it to himself. He looked at Oran and smiled falsely.

"I thank you for joining us. I think Niall and I need to talk about the options. Niall will be in contact with you once we've made our decision."

Oran and Padraig stood up. Oran nodded at Lorcan and then looked at his brother. They didn't say anything as they turned and left. Lorcan followed them out with his eyes. Then he turned and looked at Niall.

"You trust these men?" he asked.

Niall nodded at him.

"I've used them before. They're discreet so long as the money is there. They've helped break up the rabble rousers at the distillery on occasion. Never had a problem with them yet."

Lorcan looked down at his tumbler. It was nearly empty so he gave it two more fingers' worth.

"I just don't like any of these options," he said, looking back up at Niall.

"There is one last option, though you'll not like it."

"And what's that?"

"We could give the Baron his five pound a bottle that he's asking for," said Niall.

Lorcan looked at Niall as if he'd just lost his mind.

"I won't do that. Just a few months ago the Baron was content with his pound per bottle. Now that he sees the volume we're doing and the American prohibition he wants to grab five times as much. I won't stand for it. Not only is the Baron wanting five pound, but the docks on this side and the American side are taking five pound combined and Quinn won't pay more than fifteen pound a bottle. That leaves us only five pound a bottle if you care to do the math."

"I'm well aware of the math, Lorcan, but this is another option whether we like it or not."

"And I don't like it. Five pound a bottle is not much for the risk we're taking. If the authorities found out we could be shut down. You know that. We can sell it legally for almost half the five pound we're getting. I much preferred our share being nine pound. That made better business sense."

Niall took a long drink and filled up his tumbler.

"I much preferred it too. As your accountant, it made much better business sense. If I can speak openly with you, Lorcan, as your friend and your business manager."

Lorcan nodded as he took a long sip of his whisky. The chatter in the pub was loud but they did not have to lean in to hear each other.

"I think we should save ourselves the two thousand pounds and have this issue taken care of once and for all."

Lorcan grimaced and shook his head wearily.

"Just hear me out."

"Fine."

"It's less messy that way. If we try and rough him up, or God forbid his wife, which I find quite distasteful, we'll always be worried about him plotting against us."

Lorcan looked down into his tumbler, perhaps hoping it was a crystal ball with a better solution to his problems. None showed themselves.

"I say we save ourselves some money and put an end to the problem altogether. There's less chance of having Oran and his brother mixed up with the police at some stage and we'll be removed from it. I know that our man can do this efficiently, effectively and quietly. There'll never be any suspicion shone on us whatsoever."

Lorcan looked up from his tumbler and sighed. He shook his head slowly.

"That sounds all very well, but our Baron has been a key piece in getting these shipments of whisky across the pond. It's not the dock workers we need be worried about, but the government's control over the harbor. The next Lord to come into that position might not be as understanding of our situation."

Niall smiled.

"I've looked into this. In the event that anything happens to the Baron, the person most likely to be ushered into not only the harbor's portfolio but also the Lord Chancellor's position is likely to be Lord Sinjin Paussage."

"That doesn't mean anything to me," said Lorcan.

"What it means," said Niall, "is that we couldn't hope for a more influential Lord to pick up where the Baron leaves off."

"How so?"

"Paussage is a man of many indiscretions not the least of which are a thirst for whisky and philandering. We couldn't hope for a more fallible man."

Niall grinned and licked his lips. The taste of victory was seeming almost as sweet as the taste of whisky. Lorcan looked at him a long time before speaking.

"It's still risky," he said.

"As is business generally," answered Niall.

CHAPTER SEVEN

Kilburn London

"You know they've been rounding up innocent people all day these past two days," said Aidan, hardly containing the anger in his voice.

He was drinking a Guinness and he was making quick work of it. Opposite him was Cooney. Cooney nodded and sipped on a Smithwick's cream ale.

The pub was another Irish pub called The Green Emerald. It was just a few blocks away from The Loyal Beagle. It was dingier and smaller. More cramped and musty. The beer was cheaper and the crowd poorer and rougher around the edges. Mostly made up of immigrant Irish workers, Catholic to the man. They had come over to find work and for a better opportunity at the docks. They sent money home each week and each night they'd be at the pub. Sundays they'd be at church repenting for their sins of the week.

It was a raucous place and you had to talk loudly to

be heard around a table, but nobody took any notice unless you spilled a man's drink. Then it was fighting words, and if the words didn't help then the knuckles sought to be heard over the clamor. But tonight was a quieter night. The mood was far more somber, and not just at the table where Cooney and his lads sat. For word had made its way quickly to The Green Emerald that England was taking a hardline regarding Bloody Sunday.

Cooney nodded at his drink, though it was for Aidan.

"Everybody knows that, lad," he said.

Cooney was on his second ale. There'd be more to come tonight. There was a lot of thinking that needed to be thought and a lot of decisions that needed to be made. They'd been sent over here to do something about the Englishman's inability to buckle under pressure. The methods were up to him and his men. This is what they were going to have to hash out.

"Then what are we going to do about it?" asked Aidan.

"That's what we're here to decide," said Cooney.

He looked around the table somberly. He only had his most trusted men with him. Aidan Boyle, Tadgh Ahearn, Cathal McClery, Jarlath Payne and Daire Nolan. Daire Nolan was grinning at one of the waitresses at the next table. She was a short Irish lass with red hair and green eyes the color of emeralds. Perhaps that's why she'd been hired. She had caught his eye and he had caught hers.

"Daire," said Cooney, looking at him.

Tadgh inhaled on his cigarette and blew smoke at Daire. That got his attention. He waved it off and frowned at Tadgh.

"What's the meaning, Taddy?"

Taddy was a nickname that Tadgh didn't care for much. You could call him Tadgh or Tad. Hell, you could call him late for dinner, but don't call him Taddy unless you were ready to back it up with your knuckles. Daire was the kind willing to back up anything with a splash of violence. A charming, good-looking man of average height with black wavy hair and an easy smile. The same smile he'd wear dancing with an Irish lass or knocking an Englishman's teeth out of his mouth.

Tadgh nodded over at Cooney with the cigarette still stuck in his mouth.

"The boss is talking," he said.

This assuaged Daire's flared temper. He looked over at Cooney.

"Sorry, Paddy," he said, "just enjoying the view."

"We can see that. But we didn't come out to look at the lasses," said Cooney. "We've got business to take care of."

Daire nodded and took a long drink of his beer. Aidan looked hard at Daire, but Daire didn't notice. If there was one of them here up to giving Daire a go for it, it was Aidan. Other than Cooney that is.

"Give us an idea of what you think, Dairey boy," said Aidan, trying to goad him.

It wasn't hard to get on Daire's bad side, but nicknames weren't one of those ways. Daire smiled at Aidan. It was a genuine smile. He liked the man. He liked his conviction and his temper and his seriousness. More than that Daire liked the trust he could place in him.

"I say we rip the Woolsack apart," he said, grinning at Aidan still.

"The Woolsack?" asked Aidan, incredulous.

Aidan looked around with his one eyebrow cocked.

"The Woolsack. What the hell is the Woolsack?" he asked.

"The Woolsack," said Cooney, "is the cushion the Lord Chancellor sits on."

Aidan shook his head and frowned.

"Dairey boy wants to rip apart the stupid cushion the Lord Chancellor sits on? Does he even know what we're here talking about?"

"Indeed he does," said Cooney, "though his euphemism is a bit obtuse."

"English, Paddy, please."

"Daire is beating around the bush and being difficult about it," said Cooney.

All the while Daire was grinning and having a grand old time with confusing Aidan.

"I should knock some bloody sense into him is what I ought to do," said Aidan, still hot under the collar.

"Yes, I should think so," said Daire.

"Enough lads," said Cooney, "let's get on with it. Daire, what do you have in mind?"

The redheaded waitress came by and stood closer than she needed at Daire's right side. He looked up at her. Her face was the color of fresh cream with soft almost imperceptible freckles.

"Can I get you gentlemen anything else?" she asked, looking around.

Before anyone else could chime in, Cooney ordered a round of the same. His tone informed her that she wasn't welcome to dillydally. She left.

"I wanted to talk to her," said Daire, trying to inflect disappointment in his voice.

"Listen, lad, if we get done here at a reasonable time you can do what the hell you like, I don't care. But you've got a lass on the isle you seem pretty sweet on and we've got business to conduct. Now let's get to it," said Cooney.

"Fine," said Daire still smiling. He looked over at Aidan. "When I'm suggesting we should rip up the Woolsack, what I'm really saying is we should rip up the Lord Chancellor. This Baron Marphallow. Do you understand?"

"Finally," said Aidan, "you're starting to make some sense. I knew there was a reason I liked you."

Cooney shook his head.

"And I suppose we'll just head on up Bishops Avenue and knock on his door in broad daylight and get on with it then?" asked Cooney.

"Something like that. Look," said Daire. "I'm just the face for the organization, you're the brains."

"You're being a smart arse," said Cooney, "and it's trying my patience."

Cooney's eyes glinted cold and direct at Daire. He was liable to get up and punch him in the chops if Daire didn't get serious. And Daire knew it.

"Look boss," said Daire, trying placate Cooney, "we go in at night. In and out quickly. Just like that. Doesn't need to be complicated. Aidan and I can do it. No need for all of us to get involved. But we've got to cut the head off the serpent and the head is the Woolsack."

Cooney looked around, seeking any other input the others might add.

"I like it," said Tadgh.

"Me too," said Cathal.

Cooney looked at Jarlath.

"I haven't heard nothing better yet," said Jarlath.

"It's easy to like," said Cooney. "Doesn't mean it'll be easy to accomplish. Have any of you thought about the consequences?"

"The way I see it," said Jarlath, "the consequences are already happening. They're sending soldiers to our country and rooting out anyone who ever knew someone with the IRM or Ceann Daoine."

"What I'd sooner do," said Tadgh, "is blow up all the parliament buildings."

Aidan looked over at him.

"I take back every bad thing I ever said about you, Tad."

He grinned at the tall thin man with the cigarette still stuck in his mouth. The Irish lass came by with a tray of six beers. She placed them all in the middle of the table. It was every man for himself. Though it wasn't hard to figure out who was drinking what. As she turned to leave, Daire grabbed her wrist. She looked down at his hand with a cross face until she realized who it belonged to. When her eyes met his she smiled at him.

"What time do you get off, love?" he asked.

She looked him up and down. She looked at his left hand which cradled his dying beer. She didn't see a wedding ring. She liked the look of that.

"Midnight," she said.

"I'll wait for you."

She grinned and walked off with a slightly bigger bounce in her step.

"After we're done with the Woolsack, we can get going on the parliament buildings," said Daire, with renewed confidence like a puffed up peacock. Daire picked up his mug of beer and raised it to those around him.

"Sláinte chuig na fir, agus go mairfidh na mná go deo," he said.

The rest of them picked up their mugs and clinked them with each other to the loud noise of "sláinte" in unison.

"Getting back to business," said Cooney. "I'm not interested in the parliament buildings. We have what should be a very simple task before us. And yet, and yet I fear it might be unrealistically simple."

"I don't understand," said Jarlath, taking a large drink from his beer.

"I don't think it's going to be as easy as just popping by his house, whether under cover of darkness or not, and putting an end to it. I'm sure that in light of the recent events in Ireland, the English are not sparing any expense in protecting their most important politicians. And I have a suspicion that this protection will be especially enforced for the Woolsack."

The men nursed their beers and twiddled with their thoughts. Cooney had a point. The government was likely to start putting stricter security into place.

"Well, we'll just have to take a look and see," said Aidan. "We'll just spend the next couple of nights looking at the lay of the land so to speak."

"That's not a bad idea," said Tadgh.

Daire and Jarlath nodded. Cooney nodded too, slowly, staring into his mug of beer. He took a long drink. The Green Emerald was getting busy and the beer was getting warm.

"Not a bad idea lads, not a bad idea at all," he said. "Tadgh, Aidan and Daire will do the reconnaissance tomorrow. Me, Jarlath and Cathal will hold vigil over Wednesday."

The men nodded somberly. The drank their beer

and looked at the table.

"Who wants this job?" asked Cooney after some time. "I'm only allowing two of you for it."

He looked around the table at his men. He was expecting nods from each and everyone of them. That's exactly what he got. He nodded.

"I'll take Tadgh."

Tadgh grinned and put his cigarette out in the ashtray.

"I thought you said it was a two man job?" asked Aidan.

"Aye, I did, lad. And it's me and Tadgh."

"That's not right," said Aidan.

"Listen, lad, all of this lies squarely on my shoulders. I've got to be there to make sure it's done right."

"You don't trust us to get the job done," said Aidan.

Cooney grabbed his arm and looked him hard in the eye.

"I trust you, lad. Just like you're my own brother. But they want me to make sure it gets done right. If it's about the money, I'll tell all of you," and Cooney looked around the table, "that we're all going to split the bonus."

Aidan looked dejected. His shoulders slumped and his beer didn't look very refreshing to him anymore.

"No, it's not that. I just, I just wanted a go," he said.

"I know, lad," said Cooney, letting his arm go. "You'd all have been happy to step in. Am I right?"

"Aye," said Cathal.

Tadgh and Jarlath nodded.

"If I'd have to have done it, I would've," said Daire.

"I see a traitor in our midst," said Cathal, his Irish eyes glinting with delight.

Daire grinned at him and nodded.

"You're right, Cath, I'm about to see my contact in the government just after we wrap up here."

"Yeah, and who'd that be?" asked Cathal, playing along.

"You mean you couldn't have figured it out yet?"

Cathal shrugged and drank his beer.

"Why, it's our redheaded waitress all this time. I'm surprised you didn't recognize her."

Cathal shrugged his shoulders again.

"Doesn't ring a bell," he said.

"But surely you know the Baroness Strumpet... Your wife!"

Cathal laughed out loud and tossed his head back.

"You're a right tosser you are," he said.

"Back to business, lads," said Cooney before sipping his beer. "I've got a man who'll lend us some coveralls for the occasion. We're digging ditches across from the Woolsack's home in the vacant lot. Try and be discreet about it. It's more a sit, see and listen than a banging and clattering. You three," said Cooney, looking over at Tadgh, Daire and Aidan, "will start at six. That'll be around his dinner time. I want eyes up and down Bishops Avenue at least until past midnight. Is that clear?"

The three men nodded. The mood around the table had become somber.

"Alright then, lads," continued Cooney, "tomorrow morning at six you'll meet me at my room and I'll get you your coveralls."

Daire nodded into his beer and then sipped on it slowly. Savoring the flavor. Tadgh took another cigarette from his tin and lit it up. Aidan nodded with more excitement. He was eager to be involved and he wanted to make a good impression.

"Sure thing, boss, easy as can be."

"Simple, lad, never easy. Remember, you're out there in the open. If any bobbies come by you'll have a lot of explaining to do. You'll have to sell it. That's why it's best to remain unseen and leave the seeing to yourselves," said Cooney. "You understand?"

Aidan nodded less enthusiastically. Daire looked off towards the bar where the Irish waitress was collecting some drinks. If he was lucky he might have a long couple of nights ahead of him. The first one being more enjoyable than the latter.

CHAPTER EIGHT

Marphallow Home

OUTSIDE the large home Constable Devlin Pearce could hear the birds chirping. It was a sunny day in November. The sort of day that made you long for the return of spring. Though that was dreaming. Spring was further away than his salary was in allowing him to live in a place like this. The leaves on the tree outside the window were long gone. No indication of what they might even have looked like. Pearce wondered for a moment if the leaves were ovate or perhaps orbicular. Though on second thought he didn't fancy orbicular. It was a large tree, reminding him of a great oak tree, but he was fairly certain it wasn't. So that possibly ruled out palmate leaves.

Pearce felt a tap on his shoulder. He looked over and saw the Inspector.

"Are you with me, lad?" asked Inspector Rory Husher.

Pearce looked at him and nodded, smiling.

"I am, inspector."

"Could have fooled me. The body's here, lad, not outside."

Pearce nodded again and twirled his wispy mustache. Husher wondered about the young man. He didn't seem to have his mind in it. Yet he had prominently risen already in Scotland Yard to become assigned to the homicide unit.

Pearce snuck another look outside. If he were a guessing man, he liked the leaves to be ovate, perhaps with serrated edges, perhaps smooth. He pursed his lips together and nodded to himself. His father would have known. He was a gardener his whole life, until he had passed away earlier in the year.

He turned and found the Inspector bent over looking at the wound. It was Pearce's first homicide in Bishops Avenue, though not his first homicide he had investigated. He'd been in homicide since shortly after his twentieth birthday this year. He looked at the Inspector, bent over looking at the deceased with his hands clasped behind his back. The heels of his feet together and the point of his shoes separated at ninety degrees.

The Inspector was an odd looking man, but he was dedicated to his service. He was just a little taller than Pearce but much heavier. In different circumstances he might have been a boxer or wrestler. Pearce couldn't be sure. What he was sure about, was how the Inspector reminded him of a bulldog. Thick all around, with a round face and short cropped brown hair. The monocle's chain hung like a large smile from his breast pocket to his eye as he peered intently at the wound.

After some time he stood back up and looked over at Pearce who had his right arm across his chest and his left hand up against his cheek. The Inspector's one eye glowered at him through the monocle.

"So, lad, what do you make of this?" asked Inspector Husher.

"I'd say he's quite dead, sir," said Pearce without a hint of irony to his voice.

Husher turned and looked at the body again.

"Quite," he said, looking back at Pearce.

"What I mean to say, Inspector, is that it appears the letter opener was only used to stab him just that once."

The letter opener was gold with an ivory handle. The handle no longer than four inches long, and the blade itself, well the blade's length couldn't be determined at the moment.

"Once is usually enough, lad," said the Inspector.

Husher looked back at the dead man's body. Then he turned back to address Pearce.

"Do you know who he is, lad?"

"Can't say I do," said Pearce, looking over at the large, fat body that seemed eager to burst out of the black suit at any moment.

"Not much for politics then, ay?" asked Husher.

"I prefer to leave that to the liars and cheats," said Pearce earnestly.

Husher let out a loud laugh and slapped Pearce on the left shoulder. Pearce wobbled and had to take a step to his right. Pearce realized that the Inspector was not only as solid as a bulldog but just as strong.

"You're good to have around," said Husher. "That, my boy, is the Woolsack."

Pearce frowned and looked over at the body and saw neither wool nor sacking.

"The Woolsack lad, is the Government's Lord Chancellor. The man who keeps order in the House of Lords."

"I see," said Pearce, still with this left hand against his cheek.

"The man's name is Baron Christopher Marphallow."

"That explains the home then," said Pearce.

"And why there'll be a lot of pressure from up high in making sure we get to the bottom of this as quick as we can."

Pearce nodded.

"I understand."

"Also," said Husher just as there was a knock on the door. "That'll be her."

"A crime scene is no place for a woman, Inspector," said Pearce, looking over at the Baron's wife, quite distraught in the other room. Inspector Husher nodded.

"I quite agree, but she's not like any woman you've likely met. She's here to help with the case."

Pearce frowned again and this time crossed his arms in front of himself.

"Sir, I must strenuously request that we not be slowed down by a woman," said Pearce.

"You will not be slowed down, lad. If anything you might have the devil of a time keeping up." Husher looked behind him to see if the woman had come in yet. She hadn't, so he leaned in towards Pearce. "Listen, lad, this woman comes recommended from the top. She's got connections and you'll do well to offer her every courtesy if you enjoy working in homicide."

Pearce didn't say anything. Husher turned around just as Lady Marmalade was walking into the room and as the butler excused himself. Husher walked up to her and shook her hand. He led her into the main area of the room towards Constable Pearce.

"If I might introduce you to our newest and most promising member of Scotland Yard. Constable Devlin Pearce, I'd like you to meet The Most Honorable The Marchioness of Sandown."

"My Lady," said Pearce, taking Lady Marmalade's hand and shaking it as he offered her a slight bow of the head.

"Lady Marmalade, but please call me Frances."

"Thank you, Frances," said Pearce.

Pearce looked at her for a moment. He had never

met a Marchioness before, but he was certain he'd be meeting someone much older. The woman in front of him though short was barely encroaching upon forty. She was a most beautiful and striking woman with brown eyes and short curly brown hair who wore very little makeup that Pearce could tell. She also dressed conservatively with little awareness, or care, of current fashion.

Lady Marmalade turned to address the Inspector.

"Is it the Baron?" she asked.

The Inspector nodded.

"See for yourself," he said.

Lady Marmalade who had been clutching her purse in both hands walked up to the large sofa and stood over the dead Baron. She put her purse into the crook of her right elbow and peered down at his chest. There was very little blood considering what looked like a stab to the heart. She looked at the handle of the letter opener and its off white ivory handle. She looked into his inside right jacket pocket but it was empty. The outer pockets of his jacket were empty too.

To the Baron's left on a side table was a whisky tumbler now empty. There was a trace of dried powder at the bottom, and next to it was a gold tray that held a bottle of Irish Whisky. The name on the label read Red Beagle. Two small slips of paper envelopes had fallen between the table and the sofa, lying just underneath the sofa. They were only seen at an angle. Lady Marmalade stood up and turned to look at the Inspector.

"Do we know when he was found?" she asked.

Husher looked over at the grieving widow, and nodded in her direction.

"Lady Agnes Marphallow found him this morning when she came down for a late breakfast."

"What time was that?" asked Lady Marmalade.

Inspector Husher didn't have to look at his notes.

"She believes it was around nine thirty."

Lady Marmalade nodded and looked over at Lady Marphallow. There was something about her. Something common. Not that Lady Marmalade took issue with that, but clearly Lady Marphallow was not used to the lifestyle she had apparently married into.

"Have you spoken with her, Inspector?"

"Just briefly," he said, "she was quite distraught when we got here about a half hour ago, so I thought I'd give her some time."

"Where's the coroner?" asked Lady Marmalade.

"Hasn't arrived yet," said Husher, "one of my men told me that this morning was not a good morning for a murder. He's been busy with several accidental deaths as I understand it. Should be here momentarily."

Lady Marmalade smiled and nodded at him.

"It never is a good morning for a murder is it, Constable?" she said, turning to look at Pearce.

Pearce had his hands clasped behind his back. He

was looking at the large body of the deceased.

"Quite," he said, turning to look at Lady Marmalade, not sure what she meant by the statement.

"Tell me, Constable," said Lady Marmalade, "what do you make of this whole affair?"

Lady Marmalade smiled at him, but Pearce could see a cunning and intelligent twinkle in her eyes.

"Please call me Devlin," he said. "Hard to say at the moment."

Pearce smiled at her, not wanting to offer up much of anything. Mostly because he had yet to offer anything of any detail.

"Well," said Lady Marmalade, "your first impressions then, Devlin."

Pearce could tell she was determined. What he couldn't tell was whether she was trying to assess him or the crime scene. He had a suspicion it might be the former. He looked over at the body, slumped back on the couch, very much relaxed and almost peaceful if it weren't for the violence of the scene.

"Well, Frances, I have only just now come to know the importance of our victim. The Inspector informed me that Baron Marphallow is the Lord Chancellor. An important man in government and in politics. I should imagine that he's made a lot of enemies. Without much else to go on, I'd suggest that there might be some use in investigating any opposition members of the House of Lords who might have been at odds with the Baron."

Lady Marmalade nodded and smiled quietly.

"That might be a long list," she said.

"Made smaller one at a time," offered Pearce.

"Yet this murder strikes me just off the top of my head as something more intimate than a political quarrel. Perhaps more spur of the moment."

"Because of the murder weapon?" asked Pearce.

Lady Marmalade nodded.

"Or made to look that way," said Pearce.

"Perhaps."

"I like to look at each crime, especially a murder, as a painting. One starts with a blank canvas and fills in the details as one goes along. As such, my pool of suspects starts out very large. Indeed, could not your husband have had a quarrel with the deceased?"

Lady Marmalade smiled at the Constable.

"You know of my husband?"

"Indeed I do not. But naturally he would be a Lord in the House, would he not?"

"Quite correct, Devlin, though might he not be a member of the government's bench?"

"Quite possibly, indeed likely, considering they have the majority of the seats. As I said, I like to start with a blank canvas. A member of the Baron's own party might have motive."

Husher was getting furious. He was staring hotly at Pearce.

"Forgive my young colleague," Inspector Husher said, "he'll be dealt with appropriately, I can assure you."

Lady Marmalade looked back at Husher and smiled at him.

"Nonsense, Inspector, I quite like Constable Pearce's forthrightness and thoroughness. No one should be exempted from where the clues might lead."

Frances looked back at Pearce.

"If you wish to interrogate my husband, Devlin, he will make himself available to you. Though I can promise you that he was indeed home all night with me last night. As to his political leanings, he is a crossbencher."

Pearce nodded and smiled back at Lady Marmalade. She was a woman unmoved by authority or verbosity. He admired her for that.

"I meant no disrespect," he said. "Nor did I mean to suggest that your Lord Marmalade is a suspect at all."

"Of course not," said Frances. "You're just going where the clues lead. And in that vein, how did the clues lead you to my husband?"

Pearce did not have an answer for that. He looked away towards the widow.

"I think I'll go and speak with the widow myself. I haven't had the chance," he said.

"Good idea," said Lady Marmalade, "I'll join you."

Pearce curled his lips attempting a smile that ended up looking more like a snarl.

"Inspector," said Lady Marmalade, "would you let me know when the coroner arrives."

"Of course."

Frances and Devlin made their way into the other room where Agnes was looking out the window into the backyard. It was a large expanse of lime greens, ambers, saffron and the almost brown of dark goldenrod. The bushes that once held bursting blooms of flowers now clutched at emptiness like withered arthritic hands.

On the table next to Agnes was a pot of tea, container of milk and bowl of sugar. Closer to her was a teacup painted with what looked like roses. The cup was almost empty.

"May I pour you another cuppa?" asked Pearce.

Agnes looked over at him a little startled. She smiled slowly and carefully and nodded her head. Her eyes were bloodshot and her hair which was up in a bun was now more messy than it should have been for this early in the morning.

"Milk before or after?" asked Pearce, smiling warmly and oozing charm that Lady Marmalade had not seen before.

"Before," said Agnes, looking up Pearce and then drifting her stare back outside.

Pearce held the jug of milk with his right hand and poured a splash into her teacup while holding his left hand behind his back. He looked almost like a practiced butler to Lady Marmalade. Though she was fairly certain he hadn't served as a butler for he was too young.

Pearce poured in the tea and placed the pot back down.

"I'll let you sweeten it to your own liking," he said.

Agnes turned towards her mug. She took the small silver pair of tongs from the sugar bowl and plopped two sugars into the tea. She stirred the tea absentmindedly for some time. Pearce pulled out a chair to Agnes' left for Lady Marmalade. She accepted it. He took the chair to her right.

"I know this must be difficult for you," said Pearce, looking earnestly at the widow. "But we must ask you some questions if you don't mind."

Agnes nodded. She had pulled herself away from her reverie. Her eyes began to moisten so she dabbed at them with a serviette that was on her lap.

"Do you do much of the work in your garden?" asked Pearce, starting off slowly.

Agnes looked outside and shook her head.

"No. We have a gardener who comes in once a week to take care of that."

She continued to look outside, not touching her tea.

"My father was a gardener," said Pearce. "He always loved being outdoors and tending to nature."

Neither Agnes nor Lady Marmalade said anything to that.

"How long have you been married?" asked Lady Marmalade, trying to steer the conversation in the right direction.

"We just had our third anniversary this past

summer," said Agnes, feigning a smile.

Lady Marmalade nodded and gave Agnes a warm smile. Agnes glanced down at her lap and fidgeted with her fingers. Then she reached for her cup of tea, and with a trembling hand took a sip of it.

"When did you find the Baron?" asked Lady Marmalade.

Agnes didn't look at her. She stared out into the back yard and put down the cup with trembling hands. It clattered onto the saucer without spilling a drop.

"It was when I came down for breakfast this morning."

"I see, and what time was that?" asked Lady Marmalade.

"Well, like I told the Inspector, it was around nine or nine thirty. I don't really remember. I was in such shock that I didn't notice the time."

Agnes looked over at Lady Marmalade with eyebrows pinching the top of her nose.

"And what did you do once you found your husband?" asked Pearce, getting back into the conversation.

"Well, I walked up to him and lent over to kiss him on the cheek when I saw the letter opener in his chest. I screamed and very nearly feinted. Humphrey must have heard for he came rushing in to see what was going on."

"Did you call the police?" asked Pearce.

Agnes shook her head.

"No. I was very upset. You have to understand. Humphrey said he called you."

"I understand," said Pearce.

"I just don't understand why anyone would do this," said Agnes.

"That's what we will try and determine," said Lady Marmalade, trying to comfort the young woman.

Agnes picked up her cup with hands more steady, and took another sip of tea.

"I couldn't help but notice," said Frances, "that your husband seemed dressed for the day. Was he expecting anyone?"

Agnes shook her head slowly, and put down the cup.

"No," she said. "He usually sleeps down here. He finds it very difficult to sleep lying down on our bed. Sometimes he forgets to get dressed for bed. I believe those were the clothes he was wearing yesterday."

"I see," said Pearce. "Does he take any sleep aids?"

"We both use Medinal," said Agnes, smiling nervously. "I suffer quite a bit from anxiety and I couldn't sleep without it. As you can imagine, Christopher has a very stressful job and it helps him function properly after a good night's rest."

Agnes looked at her cup of tea.

"I can't believe my manners," she said. "Can I offer you some tea."

She looked up at Lady Marmalade with hopeful,

bright eyes. Lady Marmalade smiled at her and nodded her head.

"That would be lovely, dear," she said.

"And for you?" she asked the Constable.

Pearce smiled and said "no thank you."

They both waited while Agnes poured Lady Marmalade a cup of tea.

"Oops, silly me," said Agnes. "I forgot to ask you if you wanted milk first."

She smiled shyly at Frances, putting the teapot back down. She picked up the saucer and offered it to her. Agnes' hands were still not as steady as a surgeon's, but nothing spilled.

"Before or after, doesn't matter to me," said Lady Marmalade kindly, smiling at her.

Lady Marmalade poured some milk into her tea, then placed one cube of sugar, stirred it and took a sip. It was lukewarm and bitter. It had brewed for far too long. She swallowed and smiled politely, putting the cup back down on the saucer and hoping not to have to take another sip.

"Getting back to the Medinal," said Pearce, smiling at Agnes as she looked at him. "Does he prescribe himself?"

"Good heavens no," said Agnes, shaking her head vigorously. "The doctor prescribes it for both of us.

"What I meant to say was, does your husband mix the Medinal himself?"

Agnes shook her head a little more slowly this time.

"No, he usually has me put it together for him in his whisky." Agnes looked nervously back and forth between Pearce and Lady Marmalade. "I know you're not supposed to, but he complains ever so much if I don't. And I'm quite worried about his health. As you can imagine. He only gets one dose each night. That's all we both need."

"I can imagine," said Pearce, smiling curtly.

"Did your husband have any enemies?" asked Frances.

Agnes looked over at Frances and then took to fidgeting with her fingers again. She looked down at them for a short while before looking back up at Frances.

"Well, I wouldn't say enemies," she said. "But you can imagine there's been quite a few disagreements around the house and from what I've heard, related to his work."

Frances nodded.

"Anything recently that comes to mind?" she asked.

"There was a bit of a row the other night."

"And when was that?" asked Frances.

Agnes looked up at the ceiling with her head tilted towards her right shoulder. She pursed her lips.

"That would have been on Monday evening I believe."

"And who did he have the row with?" asked Frances.

"He was arguing with one of the Lords of the House," said Agnes. "I came down to say goodnight to him. When I left I could hear them arguing. It wasn't long afterwards that the Lord left."

"What was his name?" asked Pearce, taking an interest in the conversation.

Agnes wrinkled her brow for a moment.

"I don't quite recall his name. I think it was something like Lowdy or Lawty. Something like that."

Pearce shrugged his shoulders at Lady Marmalade. She looked at him and then back at Agnes.

"Might it have been Lord Loughty?" she asked.

Agnes nodded slowly and then more vigorously.

"Yes... yes, I think that was it."

"Can you describe him to me?" asked Frances.

"He was a taller, older man. Quite slender with brown hair. He had an accent. If I were to guess, I'd say it was an Irish accent."

"Did he have a beard or was he clean shaven," asked Frances.

"Clean shaven," said Agnes.

Lady Marmalade nodded and then looked at Pearce.

"That would be Lord Larmer Loughty," she said.

Frances looked back at Agnes.

"Are you sure?"

"As I described him I am. I'd recognize him too."

"You don't fancy him as the murdering type?" asked Pearce to Lady Marmalade.

"Not particularly, Devlin, but as you might know in this line of work. One can never dismiss anyone until they've been thoroughly vetted."

Pearce nodded.

"What were they fighting about?" asked Frances, turning her attention back to Agnes.

"I can't say for certain, but it sounded like they were arguing about the violence in Ireland."

Frances nodded her head.

"Was it just your husband and Lord Loughty?"

"No, there was Lord Paussage here too. Lord Loughty even threatened my husband. That's what he told me the next day."

"What did he say exactly?" asked Frances.

"He said that Loughty had punched Paussage in the face and stormed off telling my husband that it would be the death of him."

"He used those words?" asked Frances.

"That's what Christopher said."

"And what did Loughty mean by 'it' being the death of him?"

Agnes shrugged her shoulders.

"I don't know. Christopher didn't want to get into specifics but I think it must have been his stance on what to do about Ireland."

Pearce nodded and looked outside for a moment. The sky was still a painted blue. The sort of blue you'd find on sale in Dover on tourist canvasses.

"Lady Marphallow," said Pearce, looking back at her. "Did anything seem in disarray when you came in this morning? Did it look like you might have been burgled?"

Agnes shook here head and took another sip of tea.

"Not really. We don't keep many valuables down here, and I don't believe that whoever got in went upstairs... Though I haven't checked the drawer in Christopher's office. He usually keeps quite a bit of money there. I don't know why. I imagine it's just in case."

"Which drawer?" asked Pearce.

"The right one at the top as you're sitting in the chair facing the desk. The key is usually in the middle drawer of the desk."

"Who knows about that?" asked Frances.

"Just Christopher and I, I think. At least I don't know if he's told anyone else."

"Does Humphrey know?" asked Frances.

"I shouldn't think so," said Agnes. "There'd be no reason for him to have access to that sort of money."

"And how much money are we talking about?" asked Pearce.

"Never less than one hundred pounds. Sometimes twice that amount."

"I see," said Pearce.

Agnes took another sip of tea. It was tepid now, but it gave her something to do. The milk had created a thin layer that floated above the rest of the tea almost like a wafer. Agnes didn't notice. She didn't look at the tea, she only sipped it. Then she put it down again. She blinked her eyes and brought the tissue up to dab them.

"I can't believe someone would do this to my Christopher just over a hundred pounds," she said.

"We don't know that for certain dear," said Lady Marmalade, patting Agnes' leg.

Agnes looked at her and smiled weakly and nodded her head.

"Thank you," she said.

"Do you know how they might have gotten into your home?" asked Frances.

Agnes shook her head.

"I haven't really looked, but I don't think any of the windows are broken or any of the doors."

Agnes fiddled with her fingers in her lap some more.

"What is it, dear?" asked Lady Marmalade.

"I feel so foolish," she said. "I imagine they might have come in through the front door."

"I see," said Lady Marmalade.

Agnes looked at her for a moment.

"This is Bishops Avenue after all. We don't lock our doors. Perhaps we should have."

It wasn't a question, and it wasn't looking for an answer. This was 1920 after all and in one of the wealthiest parts of town. Nobody locked their doors because people just didn't walk into homes uninvited.

Pearce smiled at Lady Marmalade as Agnes stared outside absentmindedly. Perhaps he had become jaded at an early age, or perhaps it was just because of the sort of ruffians he dealt with on a daily basis, but his flat was always locked. Whether he was inside it or not. Then again, he didn't live in such elevated surroundings. It was Brixton after all, not the slums, but certainly not Bishops Avenue either.

"Agnes dear," said Lady Marmalade. "Do you have a staff besides Humphrey?"

Agnes looked over at Frances and nodded.

"Yes. I have a housekeeper and a cook. They should both be here by now," she said.

"We'll have to speak with them all if you don't mind."

Agnes nodded.

"My butler as you know is Humphrey. Humphrey Spilligan. Edith Edevane is my housekeeper and Vera Breggan is the cook. Humphrey can introduce you."

Agnes looked around for Humphrey as if to call him. He was not anywhere visible.

"Not to worry, dear," said Frances, "we'll make our own arrangements."

"We will also need to have access to their quarters," said Pearce. "Just to be sure."

Agnes looked at the Constable with wide eyes.

"You don't think one of my own staff would have done such an awful thing?"

"We won't know until we've had a chance to interview them," said Pearce. "I wander where the clues lead."

Agnes nodded her head but she was not reassured.

"You don't mind if we take a look around, do you?"

asked Frances.

Agnes shook her head.

"Not if it will help find out who did this ghastly deed."

"It all helps," said Frances.

There was a knock at the door and after a short time the door could be heard closing. Frances looked into the other room and saw the coroner walk in with his medical bag.

"If you'll excuse me," she said, getting up. "It looks like the coroner is here and I need to speak with him."

Pearce nodded and Agnes smiled at her.

CHAPTER NINE

Marphallow Home

DR. Walter Thompson was a man in his late sixties and looked like it. That was not to say that he was unhealthy or out of shape. Indeed, he was of average build and in good health, but the job had taken its toll and he looked his age. Not that anyone would say that to his face. That would be unkind. But when you're working every day with the dead, you can't help but to think of your own mortality, and such thinking has a tendency to write itself all over your face in the deep lines of the forehead and the sagging, drooping eyelids. Thompson was clean shaven except for a black pencil mustache which did not match the white of his thin combed back hair. It did not match for it was a colored mustache that looked quite odd and if you had not met him before it took you aback.

Lady Marmalade had met him before. He was a decent man and efficient at his job. He had been a coroner for the City of London well over forty years.

Indeed, it was surmised that he had never doctored a living patient, except perhaps what had to be done during medical college in order to graduate.

Frances walked into the living room where the deceased still squatted, a hulking bulk of black with gray protruding blubbery ends that were once living flesh. Thompson was speaking with Husher as Frances came in to join them. Husher turned to look at Lady Marmalade and smiled at her.

"Dr. Thompson was just apologizing for being late. Apparently, today has been quite the busy day with accidents and suicides."

Frances smiled at him.

"I'm sorry to hear that," she said.

"Not at all," replied Thompson.

"Have the two of you met?" asked the Inspector before introducing them.

"Yes," said Frances. "I've known Dr. Thompson for quite some time."

"I should say it's been fifteen years," said Thompson. "I believe the first time we met was in 1905 during the milkman murder investigation."

Frances nodded and smiled.

"You have a good memory, Walter," she said. "That does take me back a few years."

Thompson turned his attention once again to the Inspector.

"What do we have here?" he asked. "This is Baron Marphallow's house."

"Yes, and sadly the Baron has been murdered."

"I see."

Husher turned towards the body and moved closer to it with the doctor at his side. Thompson's face frowned and he shook his head.

"Good heavens," he said. "I didn't notice him right there."

Frances smiled at the coroner. He might have been thorough at his job, but he was also often absentminded. Perhaps the dead were less noticeable than the living. Thompson looked at the Baron and the letter opener stuffed in his chest. He took his time to look over the Baron's face and the rest of his body. Then Thompson looked at the Baron's watch on his left hand. He looked at his own watch and noticed they were of similar time. Thompson took note of the time which was ten forty five in the morning.

Lifting up the Baron's wrist with the watch was difficult. Thompson went to poking the Baron's body here and there. It seemed quite odd but Frances had seen it before, as had the Inspector. Thompson prodded the Baron's chest, then his abdomen, then his thighs. He leaned down and prodded the calves. He turned up the Baron's pant legs and took note of the purpled color and size of the flesh. Then he stood back up and prodded the neck and the Baron's shoulders. Thompson then turned to look at the Inspector and Lady Marmalade, just as Pearce walked in to join them.

Pearce and Thompson acknowledged each other with brief nods.

"Looks like rigor has set in quite substantially though not fully. Rigor is full in the smaller muscles. The neck, the shoulders and most of the arms. The face as you can see is quite rigid, though the thighs and chest and abdomen are showing some palpation. The blood has been pooling in the calves for some time as you can tell by the discoloration and hypostasis."

Inspector Husher nodded and Frances looked over at the Baron's lifeless corpse. She did not like the look of corpses. It was perhaps the most unpleasant part of her work.

"In my estimation, I'd put the time of death some where between ten last night and two this morning. I can't be more certain than that without checking body temperature which will have to wait until I get back to the lab. Though as is likely apparent to most of us here, this certainly looks like an unlawful killing, though I'll check for poisoning as well."

"So you'd suggest that the Baron was murdered sometime late last night or early morning with the letter opener?" asked Husher.

"I would, yes," said Thompson. "Unless something else comes to light during the autopsy."

"Thank you, doctor," said the Inspector.

"Not at all. Would there be anything else?"

"Not at the moment. Though if you can get the

results of the autopsy to me as soon as possible. Due to the nature of the deceased's business you can imagine that this has become the most pressing issue for the government, and I'd like to get to the bottom of this quickly."

"I understand, Inspector," said Thompson.

Thompson nodded to four men hanging around in the main hallway with a stretcher between them. They were covered in overalls. They came into the room as Frances, Husher, Pearce and Thompson moved out of their way. They had the devil's time moving Marphallow's corpulent body onto the stretcher and straightening it out before they left with Dr. Thompson behind them.

"I was just thinking, Inspector," said Pearce, as the three of them stood gathered together where once there had been five. "That letter opener seems like quite the feeble murder weapon. Did you notice how it was bent at the handle. A little more pressure and I'm sure it would have snapped off."

Husher nodded.

"Lady Marphallow told me that the letter opener was actually gold. 22 carat gold. Now I don't understand my gold jewelry that well, but I believe the higher the carat the softer the metal."

Husher looked at Lady Marmalade as if she might know. She nodded at him.

"Quite correct, Inspector," she said. "Pure gold is 24 carats. And pure gold is generally too soft to be used in jewelry. 22 carats is also surprisingly soft as well. I'm surprised such a soft metal would be used in a letter opener. It was probably made as a decorative piece rather than something to be used. 24 carat gold being pure would mean that 22 carat gold would be 22 out of 24 pure. That's roughly ninety percent pure. Quite soft, and not something that is generally available here in London. That purity is usually found in the Arab world."

Husher interjected.

"Yes, quite right. Lady Marphallow mentioned that her husband had bought it in India some years ago."

Frances nodded.

"And odd weapon of choice, unless one didn't know how soft it was. Or perhaps it was a crime of passion," she said.

"Most likely a crime of passion," said Husher. "Yet there is no sign of forced entry."

"Because the house was not locked at night," said Pearce.

Husher frowned.

"Was this usual or just a forgetful error?"

"Quite usual from what I gather," offered Pearce.

Husher looked over towards the other room where Agnes still sat looking out the window at the blue sky.

"Hmm, I see," he said. "Tell me, Constable, did Lady Marphallow offer any indication that they were robbed during this homicide?"

Pearce shook his head.

"She wasn't certain, but it didn't appear to her that they were, at least preliminarily."

"So perhaps it was a premeditated murder. A crime of passion then," said Husher.

"It is one possibility," said Frances. "Something worth following up upon, and yet there is one little seed of doubt that plants itself in my mind."

"And what is that?" asked the Inspector.

"One stab through the heart. Could be passion driven, and yet coldly calculated," she said.

"Or perhaps," said Pearce, "it was a murder of convenience. The burglar came in to rob them and found the Baron sleeping. Perhaps as he paced around the room looking for valuables the Baron stirred. The burglar then seized the letter opener and stabbed him fatally through the heart, and then in fear of being caught, having escalated his crime, fled the scene without taking anything with him."

"It's a working theory," said Husher.

"Worth investigating," said Frances, as she looked at Pearce. "Remember that Agnes said her husband kept quite a bit of money in his desk drawer in the office."

Pearce nodded his head.

"Well, where is that?" asked Husher.

"We haven't looked for it yet," said Lady Marmalade.

"Then we should get to it right away," said Husher, leading the three of them out of the room and down the hall into the office.

The Baron's office was as big and ostentatious as he

was. It was a dark stained teak desk that butted up right against the window and was as wide as the window sill. The chair in front of it was large enough to seat King George V and just as plush. It was apparent that the Baron was a man of large and expensive tastes. The office itself looked small but that was likely due to the imposing desk and chair.

There were bookshelves covering the rest of the walls and on the floor was a large intricately designed and handwoven Persian carpet. It was immaculate. It looked like it had never been stepped upon.

On the desk was a large map of the world in leather bindings. To the right of it was a large brass ashtray that held blocks of cigar ash. A half smoked cigar was resting in the ashtray, its end quite chewed up. A large lighter, the size of a woman's hand was to the side of the ashtray. The fuel bowl was made of crystal and the lighting end of gold. A cigar cutter, also in gold, was off to the right of the ashtray as well.

On the desk were some papers neatly stacked. Frances walked up and took a closer look. She picked them up and leafed through them. In the middle was a letter that had been handwritten. It was addressed to The Right Honorable David Lloyd George.

"Dear David,

It has come to my attention that there are men in the House who would see the government fall to terrorists. These are not our own Lords, but rather a rag tag bunch of crossbenchers and opposition members.

They would have us sit down with members of the IRM. Of course, this cannot be done. Nothing fruitful will come of it. You know my stance on this issue. Lord Paussage and the others are vehemently opposed to any negotiations by our government.

Whatever may come of me, I pray that you hold steady. Do not be persuaded by their use of violence or intimidation. Even if they bring the fight to dear old England. We will fight them back. Regardless of the casualties.

Your dear friend,

Baron Christopher Marphallow"

A fountain pen was in its holder on the left side of the table not far from the edge of the desk map. A bottle of black ink stood closed by its side. Frances picked up the fountain pen with her free hand and touched the nib as if to prick herself. That was not her purpose. She was rather testing to see if the pen was dry or freshly used. It was quite dry.

"Have a look at this letter, Inspector," said Frances, offering it up to Husher.

Husher took it and read it over before passing it on to Pearce.

"Not surprising if you've been following the politics of the land," he said.

"Except," said Frances. "This bit about 'Whatever may come of me'. Don't you find that quite ominous?"

"I do," said Pearce, finishing his reading of the letter.

"Lady Marphallow did suggest that her husband had been threatened by Lord Loughty earlier in the week."

"And we'll have a talk with him when we can," said Husher looking around the room. "Now where was this money supposed to be kept?"

Frances reached for the middle drawer right in front of the chair.

"Agnes said that the key for the right drawer where the money was kept, was kept in here," she said, opening the drawer for them to have a look in.

The drawer was as messy as the table top was clean. There were balled up pieces of paper, scissors, empty and used bottles of ink as well as nibs and fountain pens that were clearly broken. There were envelopes and a box of cigars. Frances opened up the cigar box and found it empty except for some coins from different realms. There were silver Morgan dollars and silver Standing Liberty quarters as well as silver rupees in one and five denominations.

Frances picked through the rubbish and the knickknacks in the drawer but could not find a key.

"Can't seem to find it. You might have nimble fingers, Devlin. Why don't you give it a try?" she asked.

Frances moved out of the way to let the Constable get into the drawer. After some time as he swam his hands up and down and left to right all over the drawer he too had to admit defeat.

"I believe it is not there," he said.

Frances nodded.

"Perhaps we might not need it," she said, and tried to give a tug to the top drawer on the right, where Agnes had indicated the money had been kept.

The drawer opened easily. Inside was another cigar box and sheets of paper. Other than that, the drawer was quite barren. It was only about six or seven inches high. Frances took out the cigar box and opened it up. It was empty. There was nothing in it, and nothing to give the impression that the cigar box had ever contained anything. Pearce took the cigar box from Lady Marmalade and turned it upside down and peered at it closely.

"Perhaps Lady Marphallow was misinformed," he offered.

"You're sure she said that the money was in here," asked the Inspector.

Frances and Pearce nodded.

"Quite certain," said Frances. "It has either been taken or she was indeed mistaken. I believe I need to follow up with her about it."

Frances left the study after taking the cigar box back from Pearce and headed down the hall to visit with Agnes again.

CHAPTER TEN

Marphallow Home

AGNES Marphallow had not moved. In fact if she were all white it would seem she was just a statue. Lady Marmalade walked up to her and took the same seat she had been in just before. Agnes turned to look at her and smiled. Her eyes were blood shot. It was clear she had been crying. In her hands was a balled up serviette that seemed damp in places. She was haggard. She looked like a woman who had been dragged through the outer realms of hell.

"How are you, dear?" asked Frances.

"Oh you know," said Agnes, "sometimes I feel alright, and then a wave of reality comes crashing down upon me, and I can't believe Christopher is dead. It seems so unreal. I've turned to look at the couch where he sat and he's no longer there. I wonder if perhaps I just imagined it all."

Agnes took her eyes away from Frances and looked back outside. She squeezed her eyes tight. There was a sting in her throat and her eyes were welling but she got a handle on her emotions.

"I know this is very difficult, dear. I can only imagine. If I might offer a suggestion, I feel it would be very good for you to spend some time with friends or family, at least for a few weeks while you sort through the duress."

It had dawned upon Lady Marmalade that Agnes was perhaps the prime suspect and the one who at the moment, as the information suggested, would have the most to gain. The Baron was not only a very well connected man politically, but he was also one of the richest men in London. His young wife had her life ahead of her and with new found wealth would be most desirable to many suitors. Nevertheless, Lady Marmalade was not one to jump to rash conclusions. Much further investigation was needed before Agnes could be ruled in or ruled out as a prime suspect.

The current moment required determining the validity of the money left in the cigar box and where it might have found its way if indeed it had been taken. Lady Marmalade placed the cigar box on the table. Agnes looked at it.

"You found the box where Christopher left the money," she said. "Is it all there?"

Frances shook her head.

"I'm afraid not," she said. She opened up the box to show its empty insides. "It is quite empty, Agnes. Are you certain that's where the money was kept?"

Agnes nodded her head.

"Yes, I'm absolutely certain. I had to access it just last night to take a couple of pounds from it. A charity had come by, and as much as Christopher didn't like it, I was moved by the plight of the young orphans and decided to donate two pounds to them. I told Christopher about it, and he grumbled of course, like he usually does."

"What did he say?"

"He said I was just encouraging them that's all. But he wanted to make sure that I had locked the box away. I double checked that I had. So I know it was there when I went to bed. At least it was there a few hours before."

"I see," said Frances. "Is the money kept loosely in the box?"

Agnes shook her head.

"Not at all, I mean there is usually some loose coin there, but the notes are kept tidily in an envelope in sequential order. Christopher is quite adamant about that."

Frances nodded.

"There were no coins, and no envelope. Perhaps it was all taken."

"Well, I took some of the coins," said Agnes. "I think I took a few crowns and some florins, but there were pennies, sixpence and shillings left, of that I'm fairly certain."

Frances nodded.

"Christopher didn't like keeping the pennies, he always took them on his way to work on Monday mornings and he'd toss them at the urchins he saw down by the Thames on his way to the House of Lords. It gave him great pleasure to be able to help those in need."

Frances smiled. Though she wasn't sure how tossing pennies at orphans was helping them improve their situation. Not that she was judging, though it seemed to her that the Baron could have done much more to improve the plight of the underprivileged, and from what she could tell such was not the case. It also seemed odd that he'd be upset at Agnes for donating a couple of pounds to a charity and yet he apparently found pleasure in throwing pennies at the street orphans.

"I see," said Frances. "So you're certain there would have been a collection of coins if only a few."

Agnes nodded.

"What about the notes. How much would you say was in there when you last saw the money in this box?"

"I can't say for certain," said Agnes.

Frances nodded and encouraged her to try.

"But I'd say it was likely closer to one hundred pounds than more. The envelope seemed slimmer than it often was."

"Thank you, dear, this is very helpful," said Frances. "What sort of notes were kept in the envelope. Were they larger or smaller, or an assortment of different denominations."

"If I recall correctly," said Agnes, "the notes started with the ten shilling note and went all the way to the ten pound note, though I think there were only two or maybe three of those. I can't be certain. As for the others I have no idea how many there were. I hadn't looked in the envelope for a week or more."

"You mentioned earlier," said Frances, "that the key was kept in the middle drawer of the desk. Is that correct?"

"Most certainly. You obviously found it then," said Agnes.

Lady Marmalade shook her head.

"I'm afraid not."

Agnes frowned.

"Then how did you open the drawer to retrieve the cigar box?"

"Quite easily," said Frances, "the drawer was open."

Agnes looked away and frowned at the outside world as if it had constructed a puzzling dichotomy for her.

"I see," said Agnes, looking back at Frances.

"So you are quite certain that the key was in the drawer?"

"Yes, quite. That's where I always got it from and that's where I always put it when I was done with it," she said.

"And you're certain that your staff never knew

about the money or the key?"

Agnes nodded her head adamantly.

"Yes. Quite. They weren't allowed in the study while Christopher or I were in it. And when our housekeeper needed access everything was put away. Christopher and I have always been quite clear to them that under no circumstances are they allowed to clean or otherwise access any of the drawers in the home other than the kitchen."

Frances nodded.

"I understand," she said. "Perhaps the key will come to light soon. You don't believe that any of your staff might have happened upon it, in the sense of seeing you or Christopher opening the drawer and obtaining money from the envelope?"

Agnes shrugged, slightly defeated.

"I suppose it's always possible. Though I haven't found any of my staff to be particularly nosy. I wouldn't stand for that from any of them. And neither do I believe any of them would steal any money, let alone kill Christopher."

"The two might not be related," said Frances.

"I mean," continued Agnes, "we pay them quite adequately, and none of them seem to be in any sort of trouble."

"Would you know?" asked Frances. "Do you take an interest in their day to day lives?"

"Well, no, of course not. I don't fraternize with my staff, Frances. I'm not a common woman."

Agnes sounded indignant. There was nothing wrong with being on friendly terms with one's staff, at least not in Lady Marmalade's mind. But sadly, those from the lower classes who had married into money oftentimes appeared to be in a rush to wash any stain of their birth from themselves. And this often presented in haughtiness.

"I wouldn't dare suggest that," said Frances, with her tongue in cheek, though Agnes none the wiser. "I only wonder if you might have overheard anything in your day to day activities."

Agnes shook her head.

"No. Like I said. I don't believe any of them have any cause for getting into financial trouble. I pay them well."

Frances wondered if Agnes' idea of sufficient payment was the same as hers. She was doubtful.

"Does your staff live on the premises?" asked Frances.

"No. We have a room off to the side where they can keep their belongings and take their tea. That sort of thing. But Christopher and I much preferred to have them living on their own. After all, we hardly have need for them while we sleep, and it makes me feel uncomfortable to be honest."

"I understand," said Frances. "If you don't mind, I'd like to speak with them, if that's alright?"

"Quite alright," said Agnes. "But I should think you'd be wasting your time."

"And why is that?" asked Frances as she stood up and looked down at Agnes smiling.

"Well, it's like I said, I would be mortified to think that any of my staff were capable of killing my husband, and I doubt they knew or needed to steal the money."

"Well," said Frances, "we'll see. When it comes to murder, I find that even the most unlikely of suspects can sometimes be the perpetrator of even the ghastliest crimes."

Agnes nodded and sat where she had been sitting for pretty much the whole morning.

"I know this is a terrible inconvenience for you, but we need to look around for clues and then after the coroner has finished I'll likely be out of your hair," said Frances.

Agnes nodded again and looked out absentmindedly through the window. Frances stood up and walked out and into the living room and then she took the stairs up to the main level landing. She walked down the hallway, passing a couple of rooms before she got to what looked like Agnes' room. She travelled further and at the end of the hallway was another large room, this one was clearly the Baron's. They didn't share the same room it seemed. She started with the Baron's room.

It was the largest bedroom in the house. Large windows opened up out to the back garden. The curtains were drawn, so Frances went over and opened them to let the light in. The bed was large and didn't look like it had been used the night before. This confirmed her suspicion that the Baron had not been moved, but rather killed where he had been found the next morning. The mattress was on a large iron frame with an ornate headboard.

On the left side of the bed was an intricate carpet and a bedside table with a lamp on it. There was an old cigar in an ashtray. Frances looked in the top drawer, there was a mess of papers in there. It was practically overflowing. Newspaper clippings of various international events. Old books and torn pages from notebooks. Most of them were blank or contained short sentences, what seemed like ideas or topics to be discussed in the House of Lords. Perhaps thoughts that came to the Baron in the middle of the night.

There was also an assortment of knickknacks. A dried fountain pen and some broken pencils. An eraser and marbles for whatever reason. But underneath it all, placed carefully so that it couldn't be seen were some legal documents. Frances took them out of the drawer and looked at them. They were divorce papers. Drawn up by Mr. Henry R. Travers, Esq. The Baron, so it appeared, was going to be divorcing his wife. And the grounds for it were infidelity.

Frances put the papers back into the drawer and piled everything back on top of them. The divorce papers had been signed by both the Baron and his solicitor, but not by Lady Agnes Marphallow. Frances wondered if the Lady knew about it.

Frances continued looking through the rest of the drawers and a large chest of drawers opposite the bed against the wall. There was nothing of note that stood out to her. Attached to the bedroom was a large bathroom with a tub, toilet and sink. A medicine cupboard was found to contain a variety of pills, including those for indigestion, heart and gout. A hair brush was on a small table next to the sink along with shaving soap and a safety razor. A bathrobe in a deep wine red with purple paisley patterning was tossed over the side of the bathtub and looked clean and hardly used.

Frances left the room and headed back towards Agnes'. It was a much smaller room. A room more suitable to a child. The bathroom was located across the hall. Agnes' room contained a single bed on an iron frame with silver filigree work on the headboard. The bed was made though the pillow looked firm and suggested it hadn't been used the night previous. A chest of drawers was positioned at the end of the bed next to the wall on the right as you walked in.

Frances looked through it but there was nothing of note to find, just the expected clothes. The side table contained a glass that was empty. Frances picked it up and sniffed at it. It gave no odor and seemed as if it had contained nothing much except water. Next to it was an envelope of sleeping powder. The envelope contained twenty four, so it was written on the outside. Frances counted twenty two remaining. Next to the bedside table was a dressing table with mirror.

There was a smaller round makeup mirror on a stand to the left. The whole surface of the dressing table was covered in a fine white crocheted linen. There was an assortment of makeup bottles and powders up against the mirror like a skyline of buildings. On the right side of this was an expensive perfume bottle. Its label read "Fleur de la Nuit" by Maison Tortue, and Frances knew it to be the most expensive current perfume one could buy. French of course. The bottle had been used, but only slightly. The yellow liquid was still very near the top.

Frances brought it to her nose and she could still smell the delicate floral scent. It was gorgeous. She had a bottle at home. It was amongst her most prized perfumes. She put it back down and opened up the main drawer as she sat on the cushioned bench stool in front of the dressing table. The main middle drawer contained assorted brushes and small mirrors as well as makeup pencils.

The drawer on the left contained boxes filled with jewelry. In the right drawer were assorted paperback books. Mostly romances with two Sherlock Holmes books. The one on the very top was The Valley of Fear and beneath it was His Last Bow. Frances took both of them out of the drawer and opened them up to the first page. They were both inscribed by the same person and dated from earlier in the year.

"My Darling,

Your beauty is a greater mystery than Sherlock could ever solve. I am entranced by your beauty and elegance. You are my Fleur de la Nuit.

All love,

S"

His Last Bow was similarly inscribed. Frances leafed through the romances including the popular Lord Farthington Returns Home. None of these romance novels were inscribed, though two of them contained telegrams as bookmarks.

Frances took them out and looked at them. The earlier one was dated November the 23rd.

I WILL INVESTIGATE LEGAL LIABILITIES STOP

AND LOOK WHERE ANGRY YORKSHIREMEN SIT STOP

S

The second one was dated the 26th.

IN WINTER IT LOOKS LOVELY STOP

S

They were curious telegrams and she wondered what the correspondence was about. It would difficult to surmise what with just having one half of the correspondence. Nevertheless, she put them in her coat pocket and decided to show them to Husher as well as tell him about the Baron's legal documents she had just found and the inscriptions in the book.

Frances stood up and looked around. There were a couple of watercolor paintings on the wall and at the far end opposite the dressing table was a closet. Frances took a look inside but there was nothing more than clothes in it.

Frances left the room and headed back downstairs and walked towards the kitchen. As she passed the dining area, Agnes Marphallow remained where Frances had some minutes before left her, as if she had been turned to stone by Medusa.

CHAPTER ELEVEN

Marphallow Home

THE kitchen was large and spacious. It was big enough to keep six chefs with plenty of elbow room. However, from what Lady Marmalade could tell, there was only one cook or chef, and that was Vera Breggan. However, she was not to be found in the kitchen. None of Agnes' staff were. The only one even remotely close to the kitchen was Agnes' housekeeper, Edith Edevane. Frances walked up to her as she sat at an average sized wooden table with four wooden chairs around it. Edith ate an apple from a plate that had been cut in pieces. Not the plate, it was the apple she had cut up. It was a red apple, its aromatic and slightly sweet fragrance tickled Frances' nose. Frances offered her hand.

"How do you do, I'm Frances Marmalade," she said.

Edith put down her piece of apple and wiped her hand on a serviette on her left side. She stood up and curtsied before taking Lady Marmalade's hand.

"Pleased to meet you, my Lady, I'm Edith Edevane."

Frances was briefly taken aback by the formality. The woman must have heard someone acknowledge her by her title, for she had given Edith no indication of it.

"Please call me Frances. There's no need for formality my dear. Should I call you Edith or Mrs. Edevane?"

Edith smiled a curt smile at Frances and remained standing.

"Please call me Edith."

"Edith," said Frances. "I understand that you're Lady Marphallow's housekeeper."

Edith nodded. She was a slim woman of average height. That put her a few inches taller than Lady Marmalade. She was also likely twenty years older too. Frances put her in her late fifties. She had a hard face that made her look unhappy and cross. Though Frances couldn't be certain if that was truly her personality. She hadn't known her long enough. She wore little makeup, just enough to put some color on her cheeks and her hair was short and grey. She was plain looking and from what Frances could gather, unmarried.

"Do you know where Mr. Spilligan and Mrs. Breggan are?" asked Frances.

"I should imagine they're out back having a cigarette."

Frances nodded and smiled at her. Edith gave no

smile in return, and waited until Frances had exited the room to the back garden before she sat down and continued to eat her apple. She paid no attention to what was going on outside. There was nothing to hear even if she tried. Besides which, the day had been incredibly difficult what with the death of her employer.

Outside, Frances saw Mr. Spilligan and Mrs. Breggan. They were at the end of the garden a good hundred feet away if Lady Marmalade had to guess. They both had cigarettes in their hands, though as Frances strode towards them, Mrs. Breggan snuck hers in her left hand behind her guiltily. Frances walked up to them with a pleasant non-threatening smile on her face.

"How do you do," she said, smiling at them warmly. "I'm Frances Marmalade."

Neither of them said anything for a moment. Finally, Mrs. Breggan curtsied with her left hand still behind her back.

"My Lady, I'm pleased to make your acquaintance. I'm Vera Breggan."

She looked furtively at Frances.

"Please call me Frances, dear, and please indulge in your cigarette if you wish."

"Thank you, my Lady," said Breggan, unable to use Frances' first name.

She pulled her hand out from behind her and took a puff on her cigarette. There wasn't much of it.

Humphrey Spilligan on the other hand had just started his cigarette or so it seemed. He looked at Lady Marmalade with what might have been disdain or just his height looking down at her, but she was unmoved. Spilligan took a long draw on his cigarette before speaking.

"I am Humphrey Spilligan," he said, "as I'm sure you know."

Lady Marmalade nodded, looking up at him, keeping her smile warm and friendly on her face.

"Terrible crime committed in this home," said Frances.

"Awful, my Lady," said Breggan.

Frances looked at her and nodded. Vera was a plump short woman, close to Lady Marmalade's height with rosy cheeks and a round face. Frances put her in her late twenties. She seemed like the simple sort of milkmaid you might find on a country farm. Her hair was brown and in two braids that hung down either side of her face, coming to rest a short distance above her ample bosom. She wore a grey dress that went to her calf and a white apron that had smears of pink on it. Frances assumed it was the blood of some poor beast.

"You're Lady Marphallow's cook, aren't you?" asked Frances.

"Yes ma'am," said Breggan. "She's been awful good to me."

"And how long have you been employed with the

Marphallows?"

"Five years this past spring, ma'am," said Breggan. "Best five years of my employment so far."

"You've been happy to work here?"

"Oh yes," said Breggan. "They've treated me right kind they have."

Out of the corner of her eye Frances could see the ever so slight quizzical look that Humphrey gave Vera as he looked on at the two of them talking. Humphrey Spilligan was a tall slender man in a black butler's uniform. His grey hair was parted at the side and he was clean shaven. He stood with this hands crossed in front of him with his two fingers on his right hand jutting out with the cigarette between them. The smoke curled up in front and to the side of his face. There was something about Humphrey's carriage. The way he stood and held his hands, his effete manner that suggested to Frances that he was a closeted homosexual.

"They've paid you adequately then?" asked Frances.

"Oh most certainly, my Lady," said Vera, "I really can't complain."

Lady Marmalade didn't believe her. Though to be fair, times were tough and most men and women were happy to have work whatever it might be.

"Tell me," said Frances, "did you know if Lord and Lady Marphallow kept any money in the house?"

Frances looked at Vera carefully, looking for any telltale signs that she might be lying. Vera took another puff.

"It helps calm the nerves you know," said Vera, "especially with everything that's been happening today. Quite terrible really. Terrible."

Frances nodded, unsure if Vera was stalling or just nervous. Frances didn't say anything for a long while. This made Vera even more nervous. So nervous in fact that she started to talk.

"I imagine they must keep money around, mustn't they?" she asked, looking for reassurance from Francs which she wouldn't give.

"Why would you think that?" asked Frances without judgement.

Vera looked over at Humphrey looking for some reassurance. He wouldn't offer it either.

"Well, they're rich they are. He was a baron after all, he must have some money. I mean they have a big house, and sometimes the Lady gives some to Mrs. Edevane if she asks her to pick something up from the shop."

Frances nodded.

"Yes, that would seem quite right. And do you know where Lady Marphallow might keep this money?" asked Frances.

Vera shook her head vigorously as if a bee were buzzing by looking to sting her.

"No, not at all, ma'am. I've never seen where she keeps it. Wouldn't be my business, would it?"

"No I suppose it wouldn't."

Frances turned towards Humphrey.

"And you're the butler?"

Humphrey nodded and took a puff on his cigarette. Vera put hers out on the bark of the tree behind her. She held onto the stub as if it were an injured bird.

"How long have you been with the Marphallows?"

"I should think it's been twenty years this past spring," he said. "I'll be happy to speak to the Inspector about all of this. I didn't do it."

"I didn't ask you if you had."

"But if you'll forgive me, Frances, you're being quite sharp in your questioning, and I've never heard of a police woman before."

"Then you are misinformed, Humphrey, for there are already police women patrolling the streets."

Humphrey shrugged.

"I bet there's not one woman detective constable," he said.

"And you'd be quite right. But if you are feeling awkward talking to a woman about a crime, Mr. Spilligan, I can quite easily request the Inspector come and make you more comfortable with that idea."

Frances offered him a stiff smile. They locked eyes for a moment and Frances held his gaze until he broke away and looked at his cigarette.

"No need for that," he said. "I just haven't seen it yet. I'll be happy to tell you what I know, just like I would the Inspector."

"Then we'll get along famously," said Frances. "Are

you aware of any amounts of money that your employers keep in their home?"

Humphrey shook his head.

"Not at all. But like Vera says, sometimes Lady Marphallow gives Edith some money to buy things from the store."

"What sort of things?"

Humphrey frowned.

"Odds and sods, mostly produce or some flour or sugar if Vera needs something for her cooking. Sometimes we accept parcels here and the driver needs to be paid for it. What has any of this got to do with the Baron's murder?"

"We'll have to see. Nothing is ever as it seems. I assume if you've been employed here for twenty years that you've been quite happy with the salary you've been paid."

Humphrey looked down at the ground.

"Happy enough."

"You'd like more?"

Humphrey looked up and inhaled on his cigarette. Then he turned around and rubbed it out against the trunk of the tree. He squished the bit of ash with his shoe. He dropped his stub into Vera's hand and looked back at Lady Marmalade.

"Wouldn't we all prefer a little more? Wouldn't you?"

"I'm quite happy with what I have," said Frances.

"Yes, I suppose you are," he said.

It was with a sarcastic tone he offered those words. He was a man who seemed unhappy with his lot in life. Or perhaps he was just not very responsible financially. Either way, it would offer motive.

"So you don't think that the Marphallows pay enough, do you?"

"I know they pay the going rates, Frances," said Humphrey, clearly annoyed with where this conversation was going.

"Then what are you trying to say?"

Frances looked up at the tall, thin man. He looked older than his late fifties would suggest. Frances would put him at seventy more likely. But she couldn't be sure if that was the gauntness in his face, the cigarettes he smoked or his general sense of dissatisfaction. Whatever it was, she was determined to get to the bottom of it, even if she had to strain her neck looking all the way up at him all day.

"I'm saying I'd like more, and I'm saying that I deserve more for all the years I've been in service to them."

Vera was nodding solemnly. Frances looked at her.

"You agree?"

"Well, not for myself you see, ma'am, but Mr. Spilligan here, Humphrey, really does work a lot for them and he does deserve more if he says so."

Vera looked back down at the ground, or perhaps she was looking at the two dead stubs in her hand which she held carefully. Either way, Frances found her an odd, if not simple bird. Perhaps just eager to please. Frances looked back over at Humphrey.

"Were the Baron and the Lady aware of your general dissatisfaction with your wages?" she asked him.

Humphrey looked over her head back towards the house. Perhaps he saw someone calling his name, though rather the blank stare in his eyes suggested he was thinking.

"I hadn't had a chance to mention it to the Baron. I was planning on bringing it to his attention this weekend. Today even would have been a good day to bring it up... But then you know what happened."

Not only was he riddled with general malaise, he seemed to be a coward with it too, or so thought Frances. Perhaps a sad, lonely, old homosexual bitter at life's hand that he had been dealt. Frances turned towards Vera.

"Tell me, Vera, what time were you here this morning?"

"Eight o'clock like I'm supposed."

Vera looked around nervously. Frances noticed that she didn't wear a watch.

"How can you be so certain if you don't have a watch, Vera?"

"Well, ma'am," said Vera, "I have a clock at home naturally, and I'm always awake by six in the morning on weekends. Four on weekdays. The bus and the walk to my employers' home here takes me exactly fifty seven minutes, and I leave the house promptly as my clock chimes seven. I haven't been more than five minutes late these past five years on more than three occasions. Though perhaps Lady Marphallow will know for certain. I also heard the grandfather clock in my employers' living room chime eight times shortly after I arrived."

Frances nodded.

"And what time is breakfast service on Saturday mornings?"

"Lady Marphallow likes it ready for nine, though she isn't always punctual with it, though I always have it ready by then."

"And what about the Baron?"

"We take our orders from the Lady, ma'am. Sometimes the Baron eats with her, on other occasions he isn't home."

"I see. And did you not see him in the living room this morning? And wasn't that peculiar?"

"I didn't see him, ma'am. I'm not usually in the living room, unless I'm serving guests there. Breakfasts are in the dining room where Lady Marphallow was this morning. Mrs. Edevane sets up the table and I put the service out when it's ready, usually at Mrs. Edevane's orders."

"And what time did you put it out this morning?"

"I didn't, ma'am," said Vera. "I was just about ready to. Mrs. Edevane had given me her nod which meant I was to take the service through, but then we heard the Lady scream and that put everything on hold."

France nodded her head.

"I understand. And what time was that?"

Vera looked over at Humphrey and then back at the ground.

"I don't know exactly, ma'am. Like you said, I don't have a watch. I rely on Mrs. Edevane for the timing of the services. But it was before nine thirty, but after nine."

"And how can you make that determination?" asked Frances.

"Well, like I said, I heard the chimes at eight, the one chime at half eight. Then I heard the nine chimes at nine, and then some time after that Lady Marphallow screamed and shortly after that I heard the half nine chime."

"Are you the only one here at eight on a Saturday morning."

Vera looked down and kicked at the ground with her shoe. She looked up nervously at Humphrey before looking down at the ground again.

"Well, Vera?"

"Humphrey and I are here at the same time everyday. Mrs. Edevane comes in at eight thirty on Saturdays and seven thirty on the weekdays. She's always very punctual. I've not once seen her late all my five years."

"That's very nice, Vera, and I'll ask Edith about her punctuality. What I want to know now though, is were you alone this morning at eight?"

Frances could see Humphrey looking down at Vera out of the corner of her eye. Vera looked up at Humphrey and then back at Frances. She looked as guilty as if she'd just been caught kissing in church.

"No ma'am," she mumbled.

Frances turned to look at Humphrey.

"You weren't here at your scheduled time?" she asked.

"No," he said, looking straight at her.

"And why not?"

"I wasn't feeling well."

Frances looked steadily into his eyes. She tried to give him her best school marm look, but he seemed unaffected. He was also quite a bit older than her and perhaps that was the reason for his confidence. Though if Frances were to bet, she'd likely suggest that he was just a good liar. Someone who could as easily tell a lie as the truth. Someone who might even find the lies and the truths to be but different sides of the same coin.

"Have you been feeling ill often lately."

"What does my health have to do with the murder of Baron Marphallow, Frances?" asked Humphrey, unperturbed with Lady Marmalade's station in life.

"That remains to be seen, Mr. Spilligan," said Frances. "If you're tiring of my questions I'm sure I can have the Inspector offer more comfortable conditions at the station under which to answer questions."

Humphrey looked at Frances for a moment. His hands folded in front of his chest like iron breastplates meant to keep her away.

"That won't be necessary," he said. "I have not been feeling ill lately, no."

Frances gave a curt nod of her head.

"If I was to ask you what Mrs. Edevane might have to say about her employers' generosity towards their staff what do you think she might say?"

"I wouldn't care to speculate. Besides, so long as Edith is getting more than either of us, I'm sure she'd be quite satisfied with what she considers our employers' largesse."

Frances turned towards Vera. The simple woman was staring down at her feet, or perhaps her hand which still held the two white cigarette butts in its palm like squashed white worms.

"What do you think, Vera?"

"Of what, my Lady?"

"About what I asked Humphrey?"

Vera gave a shy smile.

"I'm sorry, ma'am, but I wasn't listening."

She looked earnestly at Frances, eager to pay attention this time.

"I'd like to know what you think Mrs. Edevane would say if I asked her about the Marphallow's generosity towards their staff."

"I'm sure she thinks we get paid quite decently."

"Have you heard her say as much?"

"Oh yes, ma'am. Quite often she says to me that the Baron and Lady are quite generous. Usually around weekly pay time."

Vera smiled enthusiastically as if she'd just shared a treasured secret. Frances smiled at her.

"Before we go in, I find it only fair that I let you know that Lady Marphallow has given me permission to look through your private belongings in the home."

Frances looked from Humphrey to Vera. Vera had a look of surprise on her face, and her color had left her face. Her eyebrows inched towards each other. Humphrey on the other hand looked as unhappy as usual. He hadn't changed his expression at all.

"Why would you need to do that?" asked Vera.

"Well, Vera," said Frances, "the money that Lady Marphallow keeps in the house has gone missing."

"I see," said Vera, still not quite getting it. "Perhaps Mrs. Edevane had to spend it."

"No, Vera," said Humphrey, looking down at her like a younger sister, "they think one of us took it."

This was the first time that Frances had heard any semblance of kindness in Humphrey's voice. It appeared he had a soft spot for the cook. Vera's forehead furrowed.

"Surely not," she said.

Humphrey smiled and nodded at her.

"Surely, Lady Marmalade here thinks we're guilty as sin."

Vera turned towards Humphrey and put her left hand on his elbow. Her right still held the dead cigarette butts.

"No, I can't believe it. You would never do such a thing. I would never do such a thing."

Vera looked back towards Lady Marmalade.

"You must be mistaken, my Lady. I know for a fact that Humphrey would never do anything of the sort. And neither would I."

Frances smiled at her.

"I believe you," said Frances, and she did, insofar as she didn't think Vera would steal the money, "but this is a dreadful affair, and we must ask difficult questions and upturn horrible stones if we're to get to the truth."

Vera nodded.

"I understand," she said.

"If you'd be so kind as to show me where your personal effects are," said Frances.

Vera nodded and walked off to the side of Lady Marmalade and then towards the house. Humphrey kept her company and Lady Marmalade followed behind them. Vera was young enough to be his grandchild and almost as seemingly small next to him. He walked with his hands clasped behind his back with an ease and confidence that comes naturally to those men employed in the service of butlering.

Inside the kitchen Frances was met with Edith putting away some cutlery and crockery, including the teapot and saucers that Frances and Agnes had previously used. Edith looked at them as they came in and nodded curtly at Vera. Vera dropped the cigarette butts in the dustbin and went to the sink to wash her hands with soap.

"If it's quite alright with you," said Humphrey, "I'll be attending to Lady Marphallow unless you wish to search my clothing that I'm wearing."

It was in impertinent and inappropriate comment. One that Frances took no notice of. She merely nodded at him quietly.

"Edith will to see to what you need," he said.

And with that he left the kitchen and disappeared toward the dining room where, presumably, Lady Marphallow was still sitting as Frances had left her some time before. Edith came over to Frances and looked at her.

"What can I help you with, Frances?" she asked.

Frances looked at her and smiled.

"I'll need access to the personal belongings that you and the Marphallows' staff keep here."

Edith nodded.

"Right this way," she said.

Frances put up her finger.

"Just a moment please, Edith, I'll be getting the Inspector."

Edith stood and watched Frances leave the kitchen and return a little while later with the very handsome constable and the bulldog of an inspector.

"Alright then," said Inspector Husher in his deep police voice full of authority, "we'll be looking at your cubbyholes then."

Edith took them back to the adjacent room where Frances had first met her. It was a small room perhaps not much bigger than a drawing room, with a table and four chairs and in the two corners were two armchairs well worn but still presentable. On the one side were four wooden lockers. On each one at eye level was a metal tag with the last name of the person on it. From left to right it read, "Edevane", "Spilligan", "Breggan" and then "McCormick".

"Who's McCormick?" asked the Inspector.

"That's the gardener, Inspector," said Edith. "He only comes by once a week."

Husher nodded.

"Open them up then," he demanded.

"I only have the keys to my own," said Edith.

"Surely there must be a master set?" asked the Inspector.

Edith nodded. "I'll get it right away," she said, and left them after unlocking her own locker.

Each locker was bolted closed and a padlock was used to fasten it in place. The four padlocks looked identical except that each one had a number roughly etched into it. The numbers read one though four scratched into the padlock's body as a numeral. They were in order left to right, so that Edith's was number one and McCormick's was number four.

Inside Edith's locker was an umbrella and a pair of winter shoes. On one side hung a winter coat on a hook and on the top portion was a small shelf that held a hairbrush and a small square mirror. Husher took out the winter coat and handed it to Pearce. Pearce grabbed at it here and there, mostly around the pockets feeling for any telltale lumps of money. He found none. Though he was thorough and stuck his hands in the pockets to be sure. There was nothing of note except for a bus ticket, a lipstick and a pair of gloves stuck into one pocket. The right cuff had some sort of white powder, though the left didn't.

Pearce put the coat back on the hook as Husher went through Edevane's purse which had been hanging on the opposite hook. Edith had rejoined them by this stage, and though Frances could feel her embarrassment, it was nonetheless a necessity. Edith looked down and her cheeks were red.

"You'll pardon the intrusion," said Husher, not looking at her. Edith said nothing in return.

Husher pushed and prodded through her things in her purse. He looked through a smaller coin purse that held only a few low denomination notes and some coins. There was also a ring in the small purse with a small diamond on it. Husher did not inquire and neither did Lady Marmalade though she took notice of Edith as Husher fondled it. You could tell she was quite upset and anxious about the way he handled it roughly. Though Edith didn't appear to be married for their were no wedding or engagement rings on her finger, the diamond ring was nonetheless important to her.

CHAPTER TWELVE

Marphallow Home

HUSHER put Edith's coin purse back in her shoulder purse and put that back in the locker. There was nothing else to see inside it, so he closed it up and Edith locked it again without looking at anyone. She seemed deeply embarrassed to Lady Marmalade, over what, Frances couldn't be sure. Husher said nothing to Edith. Frances thought this was quite rude. He was making no attempt to smooth over ruffled feathers. Not that she was surprised, she had worked with Scotland Yard long enough to realize that most policemen became gruff if not downright rude after a time. She looked at Pearce who was standing off to the side now observing everyone and wondered if he would become as craggy as Husher in time. If pressed, she'd put money on it. Pearce noticed her looking at him and he smiled at her.

"Thank you for your patience, Mrs. Edevane," said Pearce, looking at her and smiling. "I trust you'll forgive the intrusion into your private affairs under the circumstances."

There was nothing she could say. It was police business after all but she was pleased with the comment nonetheless. She looked up at him quickly and nodded with a small smile on her face as fragile as a new butterfly. Frances touched her on the forearm after she had finished and gave her a comforting look.

"Nothing to be ashamed of," said Husher in his big, gruff voice, "at least you didn't murder him."

Husher wasn't looking at anyone, he was staring at the next locker. The one that had the tag with "Spilligan" on it. He nodded at the locker.

"If you don't mind," he said to Edith though not looking at her.

Edith fumbled with her keys and found the one that fit Spilligan's locker. Spilligan had not joined them, he was still with Lady Marphallow. Edith opened up the locker and holding the padlock in one hand she stepped back. Frances was to the right side of the locker and she was not tall enough to see what was on the shelf at the top of it. Pearce could see up there though and there was nothing but a box of matches and a packet of cigarettes and a comb on the shelf. In the main compartment of the locker was an umbrella on the left hand hook and a large brown overcoat on the hook inside the locker on the opposite side of the door. The bottom of the locker held a pair of rubber overshoes that were dry.

Husher reached in for the overcoat and brought it out. Stuffed into the outside breast pocket was money. It was plain to see to everyone. Husher squashed his big hands into the pocket and pulled out everything the could. He reached in further but he couldn't quite get at the bottom of the pocket.

"Can I help you, Inspector?" asked Frances.

"Can't quite reach the bottom," said Husher handing the coat over to Frances.

Husher gave the notes to Pearce and Pearce went to the table and started counting them out and lying them flat on its wooden surface. Lady Marmalade put her smaller hand into the pocket and pulled out the coins. She handed those to Husher and then reached in one more time to be sure she had collected everything which she had.

"That's all, Inspector," she said, handing Husher the coat.

Husher grabbed at the other pockets which didn't hold much. There were a pair of gloves in the right hand outer pocket and in the inside breast pocket was a leather wallet. Husher opened it up and inside were two one pound notes, a bus ticket and a photograph of two boys. Husher looked at the photograph and then placed the contents of the wallet on the table and the wallet next to the contents.

Frances looked at the two notes. They were crisp and new and looked like they had hardly been used.

She picked up the photograph. The photograph was of two boys outdoors close to a tree. The background was blurry and the boys looked to be in their early twenties though it was hard to tell. They had their arms around each other as best friends might, and they both had soft smiles on their faces. The taller boy on the right of the image as Lady Marmalade looked at it might have been a much younger Humphrey Spilligan, the resemblance was there, even if it wasn't uncanny.

Husher stood next to Pearce looking down at the money as Pearce finished off counting it. Both men were quite quiet as Pearce counted. Edith looked on in both surprise and shock. She fidgeted with the keys in her hand and swiveled the bolt of the padlock nervously. She hadn't seen such a lot of money before at one time. It looked to be more money than she made in a month. Perhaps close to what she'd make in two months.

"How much is there, Constable?" asked Husher, looking over at Pearce. Both men stood up.

"Ninety three quid, seven bob, a joey and three pennies all told."

Lady Marmalade looked down at the notes and coins on the table. They were all lined up meticulously and the coins were stacked together with their own value. Seven silver shillings all shiny atop one another, the small silver thruppence by itself and the three bronze pennies, the largest in size but smallest in value, at the end of the line three high.

The notes were also grouped according to value but fanned out so you could tell at a glance how many of each there were. There was a twenty pound white note, three ten pound white notes, seven five pound white notes, five one pound notes and six ten shilling notes. Husher looked over at a constable who had joined them in the kitchen though he stood by the doorway. Husher nodded at him and the constable nodded back. He was no doubt off to get the butler before he thought better of escaping.

"So, Inspector," said Lady Marmalade, "is it fair to say you suspect Mr. Spilligan for having stolen the money?"

Husher looked at Frances and cleared his throat sarcastically.

"I don't suspect him, Frances, I know he did it. The proof is right here on the table taken from his overcoat."

The overcoat was tossed casually over one of the wooden chairs by the table. The one closest to the Inspector.

"I see," said Frances.

Pearce looked up at Frances with his arms folded in front of him.

"You don't believe him?" he asked her.

"It's not that I don't believe the Inspector, clearly the money was in his overcoat, we all saw it. But where is the key?"

"He clearly threw it away or he put it elsewhere," said Pearce.

"Exactly," said the Inspector, "and I'll get it out of him as soon as the constable returns with him."

"Why would he do this?" asked Edith, quietly, mostly to herself.

Husher turned to look at her.

"For the money, clearly for the money," he said.

"Do you suspect him of the murder now, Inspector?" asked Frances.

Husher looked at Frances and smiled at her.

"I thought you were here to help us. You're asking an awful lot of questions without giving much information yourself."

"I'll be happy to answer any questions you might have, Inspector," said Frances.

"Good. I'll answer yours and then you'll answer mine. Agreed?"

Frances nodded.

"We clearly now have motive, what with the money found in his overcoat. He's certainly a prime suspect at this point. Like you, I remain open to the possibility that he is indeed the murderer. Although I'll be happy to entertain the idea that he might not be, that perhaps he just stole the money after the fact. A crime of opportunity if you will."

Husher looked at Lady Marmalade silently for a moment with one eyebrow raised.

"What are your thoughts on the matter?" he asked

at last.

Both he and Pearce were looking at her expectantly, leaving Edith standing like a dressed mannequin.

"Well, clearly Mr. Spilligan was quite dissatisfied with his position here and his wages. Especially his wages, though he strikes me as a man dissatisfied with life generally. And yet, ninety three pounds is hardly worth risking your career on, at least that's my impression."

"Yes, but I've seen men murdered for a lesser sum than this, Frances," offered Husher.

"As have I, Inspector. I'm happy to entertain the idea that Mr. Spilligan might have murdered the Baron for such a small amount or perhaps more likely just have stolen the money at an opportune moment."

"Then we're agreed," said the Inspector.

Frances smiled at him.

"And yet," she said. "Where is the key to the drawer where the money was kept? The money seemed hastily to have been put into his overcoat and yet the key was somehow carefully hidden. And the envelope..."

"The envelope?" asked Husher.

"Yes, Lady Marphallow said the notes were kept carefully and in order in an envelope. The notes were found loose in Mr. Spilligan's jacket. Obviously taken out of the envelope."

"The envelop might be in the dustbin," suggested Pearce. "We've yet to finish looking through the lockers and the kitchen generally. I feel confident both items will be found."

Lady Marmalade smiled and nodded at Pearce. She was just about to start speaking again when the Inspector looked up past her quizzically which turned into a scowl. Frances turned around. The constable was back without Spilligan.

"He's not in the house, Inspector," said the constable.

"What do you mean he's not in the house?" asked Husher, his voice clearly showing annoyance.

"The Lady says she hasn't seen him for some time. I have no idea where he might be. I searched the house. It appears he's vanished."

"Or more likely left, which makes him much more guilty," said the Inspector.

Husher turned around to address Edith.

"Where might he have gone?" he asked.

"I have no idea, Inspector."

"What do you mean you have no idea? You work with him for heaven's sake."

"Yes, but I don't know him that well. He does his job but he's not that friendly. Not with me anyway."

"Surely you know his home address?"

Edith nodded.

"Give it to the constable then."

Mrs. Edevane nodded and left the kitchen presumably to find pen and paper.

"Go with her," said Husher to the constable. "Get the

address and have a man stationed at the suspect's home until he is found."

The constable nodded and left after Edith. Frances looked after him. A short time later another constable arrived and after dropping an envelop on the table by the money he stood by the doorway.

Frances noticed Vera doing dishes, trying to keep herself busy. She had been all but forgotten in the intervening minutes. Frances went up to her.

"Mrs. Breggan," said the Inspector in a commanding voice, just as Frances came upon her.

She turned around and looked at the Inspector. She gave a little startle seeing Frances so close to her. Frances smiled.

"Didn't mean to startle you, my dear," said Frances.

Vera nodded at her and then looked at the Inspector and started towards him.

"Do you know where the butler, Mr. Spilligan might have headed," demanded the Inspector.

Frances joined them again.

"No... no, Inspector," she stammered.

"But you two do seem close," said Frances.

The Inspector looked at her quizzically. Frances noticed this.

"Outside earlier, when the two of you were smoking cigarettes, you seemed quite close."

"He's not like that, my Lady," she said, looking down somewhat embarrassed.

"I'm aware of that," said Frances, "I only meant that

you seemed to care for him. He might seek your confidence."

Vera looked up at her.

"Quite the opposite, my Lady," she said. "Don't get me wrong, Humphrey's very kind to me, but even after all these years I don't think I know him as much as I should. As much as I might like."

"Do you know where he lives at least?" asked the Inspector.

Vera looked over at him.

"I'm afraid I don't, Inspector. He's never me told me and I never did ask."

"You've never socialized outside of work then?" he asked.

"No sir. No, we haven't. I never been asked and I wouldn't presume to be that familiar with Humphrey," she said.

"Can you think of a reason why Mr. Spilligan might have stolen the money?" asked Lady Marmalade.

Vera couldn't help but look at the large amount of money on the table. More than she made in two months. She was sure of it. It looked awfully good to her.

"Did he take it then, my Lady?" she asked.

"It would appear that way. Are you surprised?"

"Yes ma'am. I never thought for one minute that Humphrey was unhappy with his wages. Not that I know about that, but he's always been so proper and good at his work. Like I said outside, if he thinks he deserves more then he does, but I never would've taken him for a robber."

"You mean thief," said Pearce, looking at the simple woman with neither malice nor compassion.

Vera looked at him and frowned ever so slightly, unsure of what he meant.

"No, I never did think of him as a thief, sir," she said.

"Now, listen here," said Husher getting stern in his tone. "This is serious business. There's been a murder and a theft. If you know anything at all about either, now's the time to confess. It won't get easier for you from here on out, Miss."

For a moment, Frances thought that Vera might burst into tears. But she didn't, she held onto whatever vestiges of stoicism she might have.

"But I don't know nothing, Inspector. Honest, on my mother's grave I swear to you I don't know nothing. I'd tell if I did. Honest I would."

"We'll see about that," said Husher without feeling or care. He turned to Edith. "Open her locker."

Edith did as she was told. Frances placed her hand on Vera's forearm for a moment and smiled at her. Vera smiled back shyly and then looked down at the ground. Husher took his time to look through Vera's belongings in her locker. She had an overcoat and a purse. Woolen gloves and an umbrella. There wasn't much of note in the overcoat other than bus tickets. Her purse was quite empty for a woman's. A small quantity of makeup, a mirror and some hand cream.

She also had a coin purse which was light with coins.

Husher handed it to Vera who put it away with shame, though there was nothing to be ashamed about. She tried to smooth out her overcoat as best she could. She rearranged everything in her purse. She tried valiantly to put her life back to a semblance of order. Lady Marmalade felt sorry for her. Police business was an ugly business at times.

Husher waited impatiently for Vera to finish up. When she was done, Edith closed up her locker and smiled to her. It was a knowing smile, a smile of understanding. Vera stepped back and went back to the cold sink of dishes she hadn't finished. Husher nodded at the last locker. The one that had 'McCormick' on it.

"But he hasn't been in for a few days, Inspector," said Edith.

"I am certain you're not telling me how to do my job, are you?" said Husher in his authoritarian tone.

He was becoming belligerent if not downright surly. Most likely because Spilligan had run off. Lady Marmalade didn't know him extremely well, but what she did know of him was of a man who was disciplined and used to orderly investigations. A suspect running off, well that just put a spanner in the works.

"No, not at all, Inspector. I meant no disrespect. I was just trying to help," said Edith.

"You can help by opening up the locker."

Edith's cheeks burned hot. She looked away from Husher and opened up the locker. Pearce took his turn to look inside. There was nothing there except for a dirty pair of gardening gloves and an empty tin of chewing tobacco. Pearce stepped back.

"Nothing here of note, Inspector," he said.

Husher nodded at him and looked down at the floor, rubbing his chin in thought. Pearce folded his hands in front of him and twirled absentmindedly on his mustache.

"Right," said the Inspector at last, "time to find this key and envelope before we leave."

"I'll start with the dustbin," said Pearce and he walked over towards it.

"I'll help you with the cupboards if you'd like, Inspector," said Frances.

"That would be helpful," he said without smiling at her.

Frances started at the cupboards closest to her. Edith stood around watching them investigate.

"Who has access to the cupboards?" asked Frances of Edith.

"Well, they're not locked, my Lady, so we all have access to them, though they're really Vera's domain. I can't say the last time that I've seen Humphrey in the cupboards. As for me, I'll take a look on a weekly basis for anything that needs to be replenished, and I'll access them as needed, though that's quite infrequent. Vera's in them on a daily basis."

Frances nodded and looked at the cupboard at eye level. It was filled with a variety of jars filled with flour and tins of other things. Biscuits and spices. It was quite messy, flour was spilled on the shelf.

"Is it usually this messy?" asked Frances.

Edith came around from the cupboard door to have a look. Her eyebrows knitted in frustration.

"Certainly not, my Lady, I apologize. We keep a tidier house than that."

She looked over at Vera who was finishing up dishes.

"Vera," she said sternly.

Vera turned and looked at her.

"Would you come here at once."

Vera dried off her hands on a towel and walked over to where Lady Marmalade and Edith were standing.

"Yes ma'am," said Vera.

"Why is this cupboard so filthy? You know we keep a tidy home and a tidy kitchen for the Baron and the Lady," said Edith.

"Yes ma'am," said Vera. "Sorry, ma'am, I'll clean it right away."

Vera was just about to turn to leave when Lady Marmalade stopped her.

"That's not necessary," said Frances.

Edith frowned again, prematurely aging herself with the frequency of her knitted brows. Vera went back to the dishes.

"I didn't think things were so messy here. They weren't in the other cupboards I've looked at."

Frances took down one jar of flour, the one closest, and the one that looked to be the main culprit of the mess. Through the glass it looked to be white pastry flour. Frances turned it around slowly and when she got to the side that was facing away from her she saw what she had imagined.

"Inspector," she said. "We've found what we were looking for."

Husher looked up from what he was doing while Pearce rustled around in the dustbin for a little while longer.

"What is it?" asked Husher.

"The flour, Inspector," said Frances, "it contains the key."

Pearce had found what he was looking for and joined them. Frances put the jar of flour down and opened up the lid.

"If you'd like to do the honors, Inspector," said Frances.

Husher nodded and put his meaty hand into the jar's mouth and with some difficulty with his fat fingers he pulled out the brass key. He tapped it against the side of the glass jar and it gave a dull tinkling sound. More muted than one would have suspected. Either because of the thickness of the glass or the density of the flour in it.

"Do any of you know about this?" said Husher to the

room, holding up the key like a mummified worm.

He was speaking to Vera and Edith primarily though Vera was still at the sink. Edith shook her head.

"That's the first I've seen that key, Inspector. Cross my heart."

And Edith did just that, even though she still held onto the ring of keys that opened up the lockers they had just recently looked into. Husher looked at Edith through squinty eyes for some time without saying anything. Then he turned around.

"Mrs. Breggan," he said with the same authority he had been using all day.

Vera turned around and offered him a small smile. Her hands were wet with water which she wiped across her apron.

"Yes, Inspector."

"Do you know anything about this," he asked as he waved the brass key around like a conductor.

"It is a key, Inspector," said Vera, "but I have not seen it before."

Vera was sweet if naive. Husher pointed at her with the key and then brought it in towards himself, as if he were reeling in a fish caught on the end of a line. Vera moved towards him as if attached by an invisible thread.

"Take a look at this, Mrs. Breggan. I have here a key with still some flour on it, and I have here the jar of flour within which said key was found. Found by Lady

Marmalade, I might add, who happened to ask Mrs. Edevane who uses this cupboard most, and not to my surprise she indicated you do."

Vera looked at the key and then at the jar of flour on the wooden table in the middle of the kitchen. It was upon the butcher's block which was clean and unblemished by any mark of death. Vera then looked at the open cupboard.

"I don't understand, Inspector," she said, looking quite confused. "That's not my key."

"I know it's not your key," said the Inspector. "It is the key that opened up the drawer from which Mr. Spilligan stole the money. Did you help him, Mrs. Breggan? Did you help Mr. Spilligan steal the money with the intent to take a portion for yourself?"

Vera looked down at her shoes and shook her head.

"No, Inspector. I didn't. Honest I didn't. I've never seen the key before in my life. I don't know how it got there."

Vera was on the verge of tears.

"Are you suggesting that you aren't the one who regularly uses these cupboards in this kitchen, including the cupboard where this flour was found?"

Vera looked up at him nervously. She fiddled with the apron strings that were tied in the front of her.

"Yes, Inspector. I use those cupboards. It's part of my job, but I didn't take that key. I swear to you, I've never seen it before in my life."

Lady Marmalade didn't know what to say. She

wasn't sure whether Vera had any knowledge of the key or not. She was a simple lass, but that didn't mean she was innocent. She might very well have been manipulated into doing something she wouldn't normally do.

"I'm afraid it doesn't look very good for you," said Husher. "You're going to have to come down to the station with me and answer some questions."

"But I didn't do it, I swear to you I didn't."

Vera started to sob. She was visibly upset. Pearce took her by the elbow and guided her towards the living room.

"Please let me know when you find Mr. Spilligan, Inspector. I'd like to talk with him too."

Husher nodded.

"Also, I'll let my husband know that Pearce wants to speak with him."

Husher bent down over the table and picked up the money and placed it in an envelope that another constable has brought in just recently.

"That won't be necessary," he said. "The evidence is not leading us there Frances."

Frances smiled at that.

"I will be seeking to speak with Lord Loughty about his disagreement with the Baron at some point."

"I'll be happy to arrange that for you, Inspector, if you'd like." said Frances.

Husher stood up, paused and looked at Lady Marmalade. He nodded.

"That would be fine," he said as he walked off following Pearce and Breggan. "Keep the scene undisturbed," he said while passing the constable in the doorway. The young man nodded.

Frances walked up to Edith and smiled at her.

"Quite the trying day so far."

Edith nodded.

"Why don't you sit down with me for a moment," said Frances, gesturing towards the table at the back of the kitchen where the staff sat. Edith made her way down there and sat at the table. Sitting exactly where she had sat eating an apple when Frances had first met her. Edith didn't say anything. She looked at Frances shyly and smiled at her.

"It's a lot to take in," said Frances, "but I'd like to get your take on things."

Edith shook her head slowly and clutched her hands in her lap.

"I don't know what to say really. It's an awful lot to take in."

She smiled again, thinly.

"Yes, it is. Let me ask you some bold questions then. Do you think Vera helped in stealing the money?"

Edith shrugged.

"I wouldn't have thought so. But then you see the key in the flour and she's the one who accesses the cupboards most of all. Perhaps Humphrey inspired her to do it. They spend a lot of time together smoking and chatting at the back. I think she thinks of him as a father figure."

"He was late arriving today, wasn't he?"

Edith nodded.

"He came in just after eight thirty in quite the state."

"What do you mean?"

"Well, he's usually quite well put together, but today he was distraught. Not that he'd share anything with me, he just seemed more harried than he is."

"I see. Do you think he took the money?"

Edith looked at Frances and gave a slight frown.

"It sure looks like it."

"It does look like it," said Frances, "but are you surprised? Would you be surprised to find out he did in fact take the money."

Edith shook her head.

"No. It's no secret to anyone here who takes a moment to notice that he's dissatisfied with his salary. Now, I don't know what he gets, but I'm sure he's paid the most of the three of us. You know how it is with the hierarchy of household staff."

Frances nodded encouragingly.

"But if I can speak from my own experience, and in confidence..."

Edith looked at Lady Marmalade. Lady Marmalade nodded.

"In confidence," Frances said.

"Well, the Baron and Lady Marphallow might pay the going rate, but it's certainly at the bottom end, and they don't have half the staff they need. At least not in the city here. There's an awful lot of work and expectation put upon us. And an increased salary would help."

Lady Marmalade nodded. She did find it odd that such a great house had so few staff. But then again, she was not one herself to rely on many when few would work. And of course, Lady Marmalade preferred to be self reliant. Eric would be happy to employ as many staff as she liked. But her butler and housekeeper were quite sufficient for the time being. However, they were paid at the top end, that she made sure of.

"Why do you think that is, Edith?" asked Frances.

"Why they don't pay as much as we'd like?"

Frances nodded. Edith looked down at her lap.

"I'd not wish to speak unwell of my employer," she said, looking down.

"It is not speaking poorly, Edith, if it helps us to get to the bottom of this tragedy."

Edith nodded and then looked up at Frances.

"Well, the Lady spends a lot of money, and the Baron has a gambling problem. I don't think their finances are as good as perhaps their titles and outwardly looking lifestyle might suggest."

Frances nodded.

"What sort of gambling?"

"Horses mostly. But anything that might be legal... or not. I just know he likes to gamble my Lady."

Frances had known such men before, and the

women they married. If marriage was a ship, the marriage between two such as these was a ship taking on more water than it could hold.

"You've been very helpful, Edith," said Frances, smiling at her. "One more question though. If you can consider Humphrey for stealing the money, could you also consider him for the murder?"

Edith looked up and across her face was written the plain expression of shock. Frances took that as her answer, despite what was to come from her mouth. Edith shook her head as if a fly had buzzed by.

"No, that I would be very hard pressed to believe. He's not a very manly man, if you know what I mean."

Frances knew what she meant.

"I don't quite follow," she said.

Edith looked around as if she was about to share some dirty secret.

"Everyone believes him to be a homosexual."

There were few things that Frances detested more than murder, violence and unkindness, and that was prejudice.

"You believe homosexuals are incapable of murder then?" she asked a little bit acerbically.

Edith pushed her head back and her eyes widened.

"I don't mean that. I just mean that he seems more feminine than what would be required to commit a murder."

Frances decided to let it go. The poor woman was riddled through with old and incorrect beliefs that it was no use trying to convince her otherwise. Indeed, Frances had met more than a few women who had been capable and had committed murder. Frances got up.

"Thank you, Edith, you've been most helpful. I will keep this in mind as I investigate this crime."

Edith stood up and smiled proudly. She kept smiling long after Frances had left, for she was happy to be seeing the demise of Humphrey Spilligan, a man she did not like nor care for.

CHAPTER THIRTEEN

Marmalade Park

LADY Marmalade was sitting in the living room looking out over her garden. Next to her she had a pot of tea. It was a sunny day outside and sparrows flitted from leafless tree branch to leafless tree branch. They seemed happy with their lot. Indeed, the sun seemed to cheer them up for they sang a bright song that Lady Marmalade could occasionally hear from within the comfort of Marmalade Park.

She was alone, and she reveled in the quiet time. One shouldn't say she was perfectly alone. No, Alfred was around as was her housekeeper, but for all intents and purposes she was alone. Her family was out. Eric had taken the children to Hyde Park for a Sunday stroll. Frances had elected to stay at home and contemplate the meaning of life. Though that wasn't quite true. She was home enjoying solitude. For it was within the comforting embrace of its stillness where she found the space to think upon the matters at hand. Namely, the murder that had taken up her last couple of days. On the morrow she would be bending Husher's ear. But for now, she needed to unpack the riddle.

She was certain that by tomorrow, which was Monday, that Spilligan would have been found and would likely find himself in the confines of His Majesty's bleak accommodations. But why had he run? Of course it seemed likely that he had been found redhanded with the money. But was that reason enough? Without means, how far would he get? Now if he had murdered the Baron, that would be reason to flee. But if that were the case, why even bother showing up on Saturday morning to pretend that all was well if only to run later in the day? These were the puzzles that lay strewn about in Lady Marmalade's mind.

She put her teacup to her lips and took a sip of the lemony tea. This afternoon was no time for the lazy, seductive creamy tea that she usually enjoyed on a Sunday afternoon. No, today was a day needing the more vibrant and sharper tea cut with a lemon that allowed for more detailed thought. It was still delicious though.

The sofa that she sat in was perhaps too comfortable for the mental tasks at hand. Still, it was afternoon tea and her anchovy paste sandwich was the perfect accompaniment for her tea and her solitude. Ginny, her housekeeper, always made the best sandwiches, and her fish paste versions were some of her best.

It was just after three thirty in the afternoon. An early tea, but there was nothing like a pot to help Lady Marmalade think through matters of importance. And besides, she was not known to be a stickler to routine or social etiquette, except when required in her official duties. The clock had just chimed half past the hour when she heard Eric and the children come home. That meant more tea, more sandwiches and an end to her treasured thoughts. But it was a welcome break. Perhaps taking her mind off the case would allow it the freedom to work on it subconsciously without her nagging input. She got up and went to the foyer to welcome them all home.

Declan was as handsome and as tall as his father. Only seventeen he was an apple that certainly had not fallen far from the tree. He had the same sculpted bone structure, the same blue eyes and black hair as Eric and just as clean shaven. Though he'd be hard-pressed to wear much facial hair more than the smattering that gathered at his chin and upper lip which he carefully shaved off. His cheeks were rosy and his smile as wide as the horizon.

"Hello, Mummy," he said.

Frances hugged him and kissed him on both cheeks. She took his head in her hands and smiled at him.

"Your cheeks are cold. Are you cold, darling?"

"Not at all, Mummy, Father took the rugby ball out

and we had fun throwing it to each other."

Frances smiled at him.

"He's a better rugby player than I was," said Eric.

"And that's why he's the school captain, Daddy," said Amelia as if were that obvious.

Amelia smiled up at her brother and Declan put his hand around his sister and squeezed her close.

"Amy made sure to keep score so that we played fair. Didn't she, Father?"

Eric nodded.

"Though I have a suspicion she might have given you an extra point or two."

"Did not," said Amelia very sternly. Eric smiled at her.

Alfred had joined them and was taking everyone's coat in turn and putting it away. When they were finished he turned to Lady Marmalade.

"More tea and sandwiches for everyone, my Lady?" he asked.

"Oh I should think so, thank you, Alfred," she said, and then turned to her family. "Sandwiches or scones?"

"Definitely scones, Mummy," said Declan.

"Oh yes, Mummy," said Amelia.

Alfred bowed in understanding and walked off down the hallway towards the kitchen. The rest of them made their way into the living room where Frances had just come from. Frances sat back down where she had earlier been enjoying her tea. Declan sat next to her. He was very close to his mother. Eric took his great chair as he liked to call it. It was a large wingback armchair that was well padded and had its own footstool with the same intricately patterned cloth on it. Amelia took the one next to him. Just like it though with a different pattern and without footstool.

"You should have come with us, Mummy," said Amelia. "It was an awful lot of fun. And quite a lot of people out considering."

"Well, it was the perfect day for it," said Frances. "I would have loved to have joined you my dear, but I needed this peace and quiet for this case I'm working on."

"Why do you do it, Mummy? It's awful work. I just can't imagine?" said Declan. "Oh, the horrors."

And he put the back of his hand against his forehead in very dramatic style. Frances swiped at him with the back of her hand, smiling at him. Declan grinned at his sister.

"You shouldn't joke about that sort of thing, son," said Eric. "It is a dreadful business, and not something that should be taken lightly. But your mother's good at it."

"How did you get into it, Mummy?" asked Declan.

"It was shortly after you were born, darling. I had popped over to the neighbors to borrow some sugar and I found her dead. It was dreadful."

"And did you find out who did it?" he asked.

Frances nodded.

"I did. I helped the police with it and he's still in jail to this day.

"So you could say I fell into it. Not by choice, but I am good at it and if it helps to make the world a little safer and a little better, which I hope it does, then I'm happy to do it."

"But it must be so ghastly, Mummy," said Amelia.

Frances nodded at her daughter.

"It is, my darling. Sometimes anyway, but I try not to look at it like that. I try to put it in the perspective of a puzzle. How can I best help the victim or those left behind? How can I get justice?"

Ginny came in with a silver tray containing another teapot and three teacups. There was a also a sugar bowl and a fresh carafe of milk. Only Frances had cream in her tea, and she was drinking hers with lemon. There was also a freshly cut lemon with its yellow wedges arranged in a circle. Ginny put the tray on the larger table that was between everyone.

"Would you like me to pour, my Lady?" she asked Frances.

"No thank you, Ginny, we'll manage just fine."

Ginny nodded and moved out of the way, as Alfred passed by her and placed another silver serving tray on the table with half a dozen scones freshly halved and warm. You could see the tendrils of heat twirling up from them. There was a dish of butter, a bowl of thickly peaked clotted cream and another bowl of deeply red and shiny strawberry jam. Declan leaned in. He was a young man with a young man's appetite and he was ready to indulge. Eric saw him.

"Let your mother and sister go first, Dec," said Eric smiling at him.

Declan nodded and swallowed.

"Of course, Father," he said.

Amelia waited for her mother. Frances only topped up her tea and squeezed some lemon in it. She still had half a fish paste sandwich left to eat and that didn't seem appetizing along with a   scone and strawberry jam. Amelia took half a scone and spread a thick layer of clotted cream on it. Atop that she ladled a generous dollop of strawberry jam.

"Is this our clotted cream, Mummy?" she asked.

At the turn of the century, a year or so before Frances met him, Eric had bought a farm in Cornwall. He thought he might fancy farming in his later years, but that had yet to happen. However, the farm had become a comforting place for him to nurture his wounds in 1902 when he got back from The Boer War. Like much of what Eric did, it was extravagant. A large one thousand acre farm. One of the biggest at the time in Cornwall and still run by the family that Eric had employed when he bought it. It provided some produce but mostly meat and dairy and eggs for both Marmalade Park in London and Avalon at Ambleside in the Lake District. Though Avalon at Ambleside was also fully staffed and functioning as a small allotment year round.

"It is our cream," said Frances. "Do you like it, my darling?"

Amelia nodded as she chewed a bite of her scone.

"It always tastes so much better."

Declan put two half scones on his plate and slathered them both with cream and jam. He'd be finished with both halves before his sister had finished her one half. He also poured himself a cup of tea and added two sugars and milk to it. Eric ate one half of a scone with cream and jam and had his tea as he always liked it. With lemon.

"How is this latest case going, my love?" asked Eric as he held his scone hovering above the plate in his other hand.

"Well, it's dreadful, it really is. A horrible murder and a horrible death. Then the stolen money and the suspect gone into hiding, though I'm sure by tomorrow the police will have captured him. Inspector Husher seems like the no nonsense sort."

"Tell us about it, Mummy," said Declan.

Frances looked over at him and smiled. She took a sip of tea before continuing. Declan was finishing his scones.

"Well he was a friend of your father's," she said.

Eric interjected.

"Let's not be too generous with the dead," he said. "He was a peer. A colleague, if you will, though an unlikeable man."

"One shouldn't speak ill of the dead, my dear," said

Frances teasingly.

"Is it ill even if true?" he asked.

Frances said nothing.

"It's this Baron Marphallow, isn't it?" asked Declan. "The one I read about in the paper. It's made a big splash already."

"Well, he was an important man and this is a tragic and shocking case."

Declan was intrigued. He had the teenage boyish interest in the macabre.

"How was he murdered. Can you say?" he asked.

"Now, now, Dec," said Eric, "no need to seek the grizzly details."

"I'd rather not know," said Amelia, "for I shan't be able to get it out of my head if you tell."

Frances smiled at her daughter.

"Not to worry, my darling, I won't tell and it's not important."

"So who did it then, Mummy?" asked Declan.

"This is the puzzle over which I'm trying to make sense," she said. "I can't tell at the moment. I don't have all the pieces and it's in the very early stages."

"Can you tell if it was a man or a woman?" asked Declan.

"Wouldn't be a woman," said Amelia as if stating the obvious. "Women aren't as uncivilized."

Declan looked at his sister and thought about answering her, but then he saw the scones and decided to help himself to two of those instead.

"Not quite true, darling," said Frances. "Women are quite as capable of men at committing murder, they just don't do it as often. In this instance, although the method was violent and suggests a male suspect, I'm not willing to rule out a woman either."

Amelia didn't say anything to that. She popped the last bit of her scone into her mouth and chewed on it thoughtfully.

"Well," said Declan as he thought about stuffing a bite of scone into his mouth, but stopped to speak, "if he's a politician then there will be a lot of people who want him dead I should think."

"Speaking of that," said Frances, looking over at her husband, "Inspector Husher wants to have a word with Larmer as soon as is convenient."

Eric nodded.

"I'll let him know first thing tomorrow."

"Not Lord Loughty," said Amelia. "I can't imagine him murdering anyone."

"Nor I," said Frances.

"But he is quite gruff and stern sometimes isn't he, Father?" asked Declan.

Eric nodded.

"He's a principled man who doesn't suffer fools easily," said Eric. "Though he's smarter than to commit murder. I doubt he'd do it."

They all looked at Frances for agreement.

"Personal feelings aside," she said, "in cases such as these, one must follow the evidence."

"So there is something to suggest he might be involved then?" asked Declan.

"I can't say anymore, dear," said Frances. "I hope not and I'm keeping an open mind. Time and evidence will bring to light the killer."

CHAPTER FOURTEEN

Scotland Yard

INSPECTOR Husher had telephoned Lady Marmalade at shortly before noon on Monday the 29th of November. Spilligan had been picked up and Husher had invited Lady Marmalade down to the station to take part in the interview. If Lady Marmalade didn't know any better, she would have thought that Husher might have been gloating and feeling confident in his ability to extract not only a confession regarding the theft but also of the murder.

Frances was at home alone, having recently finished some tea to herself. Alfred and Ginny were there of course, but Eric was at work and Amelia and Declan at school. Husher was sending a police car around to pick her up. He said it wouldn't be more than ten minutes and he was right. By the time Lady Marmalade had managed to freshen up, get a raincoat and umbrella ready, she heard a knock at the door.

Alfred answered the door and invited the constable into the foyer to wait.

Alfred came and found Frances in the living room staring outside through the window, watching birds flit from branch to branch. Little brown sparrows no larger than her fist. She was contemplating the fragility of life when Alfred interrupted.

"I have a Constable Pearce here for you, my Lady."

Frances turned around and smiled at him.

"Thank you, Alfred."

He walked with her back to the entrance where Pearce nodded at her in acknowledgement. He was also holding an umbrella which he hadn't used for himself as his hat was still wet from the light rain outside.

"Would you like me to call for you, my Lady, at a certain time?" asked Alfred.

"That won't be necessary," said Pearce. "I'll be sure she gets back when we're done."

Alfred looked at him for a brief moment, sharply, before looking back at Frances. Frances smiled.

"I'll be in good hands with Constable Pearce," she said. "If I need a ride, I'll call home."

"Very good, my Lady," he said.

Frances stepped out of the house and opened up her umbrella. Pearce, who had brought the umbrella for her, now kept it closed. Alfred watched them down the walkway and closed the door once Lady Marmalade was safely in the passenger seat of the police car which Pearce had opened for her and closed after.

They drove towards Scotland Yard in silence for a while. Lady Marmalade enjoying the ride and the scenery. She had been to Scotland Yard on several occasions and it was her wish that at some point during her career, so long as she was able to continue helping them, that she would uncover the mystery behind what had become known as the Whitehall Mystery. The uncovered, murdered remains of a woman found at the site of Scotland Yard. The irony of this unsolved murder was not lost on those who had a distaste for police generally.

"Has he been cooperative?" asked Frances at last.

Pearce didn't look at her, he continued to keep his eye on traffic and the road ahead of him.

"I can't say for certain, Frances," he said. "He had just been picked up and brought in when I was sent to collect you."

"Do you think he did it?" asked Frances.

"Did which part?" asked Pearce.

"Either, both, neither," she said.

Pearce sighed, and didn't answer right away. He kept his gaze forward. Frances looked at him steadily. He was thinking carefully over his choice of words.

"I am nothing if I am not the epitome of discretion," she said.

She had a feeling that Pearce was a man who took the chain of command seriously and who was inclined not to speak out of turn if he could help it. About his superiors, but perhaps also about anyone generally. He looked over at her for what seemed like a long second. Their eyes locked. Then he looked away.

"Very well," he said. "I will take a chance with you, Frances, because I think you're a reasonable woman, and someone who does this kind of work out of a fidelity for justice and a love of humanity."

That was well said, thought Frances.

"If we are able to speak clearly, Devlin, and openly and honestly," she said, "I should think that crimes would be more quickly and succinctly brought to justice."

Pearce nodded.

"Neither," he said.

"I beg your pardon?" asked Lady Marmalade.

"The answer to your question. I don't believe he committed either crime."

Frances nodded.

"In that we are in agreement, Devlin."

Pearce looked over at Frances briefly with what looked like the smallest sliver of a smile.

"The Inspector is convinced otherwise," he said. "I don't think it's a reach that he's looking to convict the butler on the murder charge too."

"I see no evidence for that," said Frances.

"You don't need evidence," said Pearce, "when a confession will do."

"Do you think he'll confess?"

"Rory has been successful in obtaining confessions before. He has a way. Especially when left to himself."

"I see," said Frances, a little worried.

They remained in silence again for a short while before Pearce spoke.

"Do you have any suspects in mind?" he asked, looking straight ahead. The windscreen wipers slowly saluting back and forth all the while clearing the windshield from the light rain.

"I haven't met enough people yet. I can't see any of the staff doing it, though you never know."

"What about the wife?" asked Pearce.

Frances looked over at him but didn't say anything for a moment. Then she looked straight ahead again.

"You believe women are capable of violent murder?"

"I know they are... as should you."

Pearce looked at her for a brief moment before turning back to watch the road.

"It is refreshing to hear someone like yourself being so clear minded. Perhaps it is the younger generation," said Frances.

"Or perhaps I like to keep an open mind in investigations and not let my prejudices blind me."

"I don't know about the wife yet," said Frances. "I don't have enough information on that relationship yet."

Pearce didn't speak for a while again, then he cleared his throat.

"I have heard that the Marphallows were not necessarily all they appeared to be," he said.

"I had heard the same."

"From who?"

"The housekeeper, Edith," said Frances.

Pearce nodded at the windshield.

"Where did you hear about it?"

"I prefer to keep my sources confidential. People don't have a tendency to trust loose lips."

Frances nodded but didn't say anything. She liked this young constable the more time she spent with him.

"What have you heard exactly?" asked Frances.

"That the Baron has financial troubles and there is suspicion he is involved in illegally selling whisky into the United States. Additionally, I hear that he is a bit of a gambler."

"The gambling bit I knew about," said Frances. "The liquor selling is news to me."

Pearce grunted or cleared his throat. It was hard to tell which.

"And his wife is much younger than him. Rumor suggests that they have not been intimate in years, and I'm inclined to believe it."

"It wouldn't surprise me," said Frances. "Are there any rumors that Lady Marphallow has other suitors?"

"In their circles it seems quite well known that she is a... if I can be indelicate, a loose woman," said Pearce.

"If that's the case, then the Baron was probably quite aware. Perhaps it was something that was tolerated."

"Perhaps," said Pearce, "yet it is my suspicion that these things can often turn sour at a moment's notice. Don't forget that the Baron was drugged that evening with sleeping powder. He would be easy to murder by man or woman."

Frances nodded again.

"That is quite true, though we're missing the big piece of the puzzle if that is the case."

"Which is?"

"Motive."

"Which will come if we continue to move in the right direction."

"It's sounding to me, Devlin, that you're almost convinced she did it already."

Pearce looked over at her and smiled. He shook his head.

"Not at all, just trying to tease the pieces apart. Until I've ruled her out, she remains on my list of suspects."

"I see, and are there others?"

"Of course," said Pearce.

"Would you enlighten me?"

"I thought you were supposed to be helping us, not the other way round."

Frances smiled.

"I am helping you."

Pearce didn't say anything for a while.

"Spilligan the butler. Mrs. Edevane the housekeeper. Mrs. Breggan the cook. Not to overlook Lord Loughty or Paussage either, and then of course there might be something rotten underfoot with the Baron's involvement in illegal bootlegging."

"Then you and I are in agreement. Those are the suspects I have in mind. But first we need to gather information, and I have a suspicion that Humphrey will be a very good place to start."

In the distance, standing like squat blocks overlooking the Thames, Frances saw the red bricked buildings of Scotland Yard. Two twins with the same austere exterior and dark grey peaked roofs. As dry and dreary as government buildings could be. Pearce crossed over Westminster Bridge and headed towards them.

He parked right outside and got out. By the time he had gotten around to Lady Marmalade's side, she had helped herself out of the car. He closed the door behind her. The rain had slowed to a drizzle so light and small that it might have been mistaken for a damp fog, or the snout of a poodle.

Pearce led the way into the first of the two buildings and Frances followed. He was quick of step and Frances had to move to keep up with him. There was no stopping at the front desk, for Pearce knew exactly where he was going. Down the long hallway and at the end they took a left turn. In the middle of this new corridor on the right was the interrogation room. A constable stood guard outside. Pearce walked past him and looked through the glass window and inside. Spilligan sat at a wooden desk by himself. He wore the same uniform that he had worn on the Saturday when Frances had seen him. It was not quite as clean nor quite as pressed as it had been then. He was smoking a cigarette and a round tin ashtray was in the middle of the table. Spilligan inhaled nervously. Pearce turned towards the constable.

"Inspector in his office then?" he asked.

"I don't know, Devlin, he didn't say."

Pearce nodded curtly and turned to Lady Marmalade.

"Come with me, I think I know where the Inspector is," he said.

Frances followed him in the direction they had headed towards the cell. They turned left again at the end of the hall, now heading towards the entrance in a U shape they had just traversed. About a quarter of the way up Pearce turned right into a small office. Frances followed.

"Inspector," said Pearce.

Husher was standing behind his desk with a telephone in his hand. He looked up as the two of them walked in.

"I've just been informed that they've picked up Aidan Boyle. He was found loitering around the Marphallow home the night of the murder."

"Aidan Boyle," repeated Pearce. "I know that name."

"You ought to lad, his one of those men involved with the Irish Republican Militia."

"Weren't they responsible for the Bloody Sunday massacre?" asked Frances.

"Quite correct," said Husher, "and now we've got one of them. Shouldn't take much to get some of the others."

"You said he had been picked up for loitering around the Marphallow residence."

Husher nodded.

"Has he been in police custody since then?"

"Good heaven's no," said Husher. "They lost him in a foot chase when they were confronted. He just happened to have been picked up this morning at a local pub. Shall we?"

Husher walked towards them as Pearce and then Frances walked out into the hallway. They followed Husher down the hallway, back towards the room that held Spilligan. Husher paused outside the door.

"This is going to be easy," he said. A twinkle in his eye.

The constable unlocked the door and they walked into the room. There were only two wooden chairs across from Spilligan. Pearce offered one to Frances and took the other one to himself. Husher preferred to stand and stood to the left side of Spilligan, on Pearce's right.

"Why did you steal the money?" he asked.

Spilligan had by this time finished his cigarette. It was a bent white spine in the ashtray with mounds of ash. He looked up at the Inspector defiantly. His hands across his chest.

"I didn't steal it."

"Then how was it found in your overcoat?"

"Somebody must have put it there."

"You have an answer for everything do you?"

Spilligan didn't say anything. His demeanor was starting to crack. Fatigue was beginning to set in. Husher kept his eyes on him. He stared at him. Spilligan wouldn't look at him. Husher sat down on the side of the table, close to Spilligan and leaned in towards him.

"Why did you kill him?" asked Husher, leaning in and staring.

You could tell this was making Spilligan uncomfortable. He leaned as far back as he could, looking down into his lap. He looked up furtively at the Inspector.

"I didn't kill him."

"Innocent men don't run from the police."

"I..."

Husher waited and stared continuously at the the butler. He was used to dealing with murderers and thieves and this man in front of him was no different. Spilligan remained silent.

"You'll be going to the gallows when I'm done with you," said Husher.

Spilligan looked up clearly quite upset at this point.

"I didn't kill him. I swear to you. You won't find my fingerprints on the letter opener."

"Because you cleaned it off, coldblooded murderer as you are," said Husher.

"How did you know it was a letter opener?" asked Pearce coldly.

Spilligan looked up at him almost in relief to hear someone else speak. Someone else to talk to.

"When Lady Marphallow came downstairs and saw him dead she shrieked and I went rushing in to help her. I saw him sitting there in that couch with that letter opener sticking out of his chest."

Spilligan looked down again, clearly upset by the recent resurfacing of the image.

"You were late in arriving to work on that Saturday. You were found with the stolen money in your jacket. You ran at the first opportunity and you expect us to believe that you're an innocent party to all of this?" asked Husher.

Spilligan fiddled with his fingers. He likely wanted another cigarette, but he didn't have the courage to ask.

"I know it looks bad," he said. "All I can say is I didn't do it."

Husher was clearly getting frustrated. He stood up and walked behind Spilligan, making the butler even more nervous than he already was.

"Doesn't matter," said Husher, "I think we have

enough to get you to the gallows."

Husher put his hand firmly, and quickly on Spilligan's shoulder. Spilligan almost jumped out of his seat. Frances was not pleased with the amount of contact nor the bullheaded questioning of Husher but she hadn't seen anything outrightly inappropriate. Spilligan fiddled with his fingers. Husher kept his hand on the butler's shoulder. Frances watched silently.

"How do you suppose the money got into your overcoat Mr. Spilligan?" asked Frances, trying a different approach.

He looked up at her worriedly.

"Do you believe me?" he asked.

"I have not made up my mind yet," said Frances. "Though I am willing to hear you out, if you can offer explanation."

Husher took his hand off Spilligan and walked round to the front of the desk again and stood slightly behind Pearce's right shoulder. He looked unwaveringly at the butler, though the butler did not meet his gaze.

"I cannot say, for I didn't see anyone put the money there."

He looked down and his face looked more ashen than it had before.

"I can tell you that the money was not in my jacket when I arrived at work that morning. It must have been put in there that morning."

"By whom?" asked Frances.

"Could have been anyone. It's no secret where the keys to the lockers are kept. Edith has access to them of course, but both Vera and I know where they are kept. And of course Lady Marphallow."

"You're suggesting that the Lady of the house would have put that money in your pocket to frame you?" asked Husher, his voice loud and obnoxious.

Spilligan looked up at him furtively and shook his head slowly.

"Not at all, Inspector. I would never suggest that. But I wouldn't put it past Edith, the housekeeper. There's no love lost between the two of us."

"Why is that?" asked Frances.

Spilligan shrugged without looking at anyone.

"I guess she just doesn't like me. We're a small group and I'm in charge, but she doesn't like to take orders from me. She always makes a big production out of anything I do. Been like that for years."

"Alright, let's pretend that she did in fact put the money in your pocket," said Pearce. "How did she know about it?"

"It's not secret that they kept a few pounds in the Baron's office," said Spilligan.

Frances was getting the impression that Spilligan wasn't being as forthcoming as he might otherwise be. And she had a suspicion as to why that might be.

"Mr. Spilligan," said Frances, sternly. Spilligan looked up at her. "I have the distinct impression that you're toying with us and offering us half truths and foggy interpretations."

"But I..." he said, but Frances cut him off.

"You have no friends left, Humphrey," she continued. "The Inspector and the Constable are convinced you're good for at least the theft if not the murder."

Spilligan started to open his mouth in protest but stopped. Frances knew that Pearce was open minded, but she was playing an angle.

"I might be the only ally you have, and my patience is being sorely tried. You say there is no love lost between you and Edith. I daresay that if push comes to shove that Inspector Husher might have Vera turned against you in no time at all."

That seemed to hit the mark. Spilligan looked up at Husher with anger in his eyes.

"Lady Marphallow might no longer require your services even if you didn't steal the money. You are tainted with shame, Mr. Spilligan and I might be your only friend. I'm certainly the only one here who might be able to find you another position. If... If you decide to be more forthcoming."

Spilligan looked at her and shook his head wearily and slowly. He looked defeated. A man lost and forgotten, perhaps even tossed aside by the hardships of life.

"I can't," he said, almost in tears. "You wouldn't understand."

He fell silent. Frances looked at him. She did understand. She looked at Husher and then at Pearce. Husher certainly wouldn't understand. Pearce she wasn't sure about.

"But I wouldn't steal a hundred pounds or whatever it was. That's not even two month's salary. It would be foolish."

Frances looked back at Husher.

"Perhaps, Inspector," she said, "you could give Spilligan and I a moment to talk privately. I think he might be more forthcoming then."

Husher looked at her and raised an eyebrow.

"I should think not," he said. "If this nancy or bum boy is unable to speak plainly in the accompaniment of the police he deserves what's coming."

"Inspector," said Frances, her voice rising as her temperature did. "I'll not stand to listen to your prejudice nor homophobic diatribe regardless of whether the subject of such hatred is a suspect or an innocent man."

Frances stared at him squarely in the eye for a long time until he finally looked away.

"Do you think I made it to Inspector of homicide by chance?" asked Husher, looking at Spilligan. Spilligan didn't look at him.

"It was not by chance but because of my skill at the job. You think I don't know about your ten pound fine for gross indecency? But that's not why you're here. We can take care of that later. But if you don't start speaking quickly and forthrightly like Lady Marmalade asked, then your fine is going to be the least of your worries."

Spilligan was clearly ashamed. His face had gone deep red and he looked smaller than he had before. His shoulders more rounded. His whole body slumped.

"I'll take care of the fine, Inspector," said Frances.

"He's lucky that's all he got. If it'd been up to me..."

Husher spat out those words to nobody in particular.

"His Majesty's Government has no business in the goings on between two consenting people regardless of religious or societal morals," said Frances directly at the Inspector, though Husher did not look back at her.

Pearce didn't have a horse in this race. He didn't understand homosexuals though he held no ill will between two men or two women who chose each either. He would however, be sure to uphold the law until such time as it was changed.

"Nevertheless," said Frances, looking back at Spilligan. "We are not here on issues of morality nor gross indecency. We're here to bring to justice the murderer of Baron Marphallow and the thief of the Baron's stolen money. And you, Mr. Spilligan, are in a position to help us with that if you'll be more forthcoming."

Spilligan looked up at Frances. After some time he

nodded slowly.

"Very well," he said. "I suppose it's all out in the open now. Now need to hide it any more."

"And is that why you ran?" asked Frances.

Spilligan nodded.

"There's a warrant out for me for that fine that I haven't been able to pay. I've been meaning to, it's just been difficult scraping the money together."

"Then you should have thought twice about being in that club when you were caught," said Husher.

Frances bit her tongue. She wasn't going to get into it with the Inspector. They had a murder to solve after all. Spilligan also kept quiet.

"Never mind about that, Humphrey," said Frances. "I'll clear that up on your behalf. What is more important right now is trying to understand who might have killed the Baron."

Humphrey looked up at Frances and smiled shyly, briefly.

"You said that it was no secret that the Baron and Lady Marphallow kept some money in the house. How did you know this?"

"A couple of reasons," said Spilligan. "Lady Marphallow would give Edith money now and then when she needed her to pick up some items at the store. Though perhaps, more obviously, they fought about it quite openly."

"About the money?" asked Frances.

Spilligan nodded.

"He complained that she spent the money too easily. She complained that he gambled too much. He swore he'd get rid of the money they kept in the house. She got hysterical about it saying how much she needed for running the house. He made her swear to keep her spending down and she promised to. This happened probably on the fortnight. Almost like clockwork."

"Tell me about his gambling," said Pearce. "What sort of gambling and how much?"

Spilligan looked at Pearce and shrugged his head.

"I don't know for certain. He was fond of the horses. Quite a big spender from what I overheard."

"What particularly did you overhear?" asked Pearce.

"Well, one time it sounded like Lady Marphallow confronted him about having been approached by a man at the market. She was obviously upset by the whole incident. She told him that this man had told her that they wanted the Baron's debt paid back. She was pleading with him to stop the madness, telling him that someone was likely to be hurt because of his twenty thousand pound debt."

"Twenty thousand pounds. Is that quite correct?" asked Husher, quite astonished.

"Yes, I believe so, Inspector. He told her no one was going to threaten him or his wife and that he'd see to it. She just wanted him to stop gambling. He told her he wasn't going to be bullied by petty thugs."

"Twenty thousand pounds is not available to petty thugs," said Husher for everyone's interest. "Did she say who these men were?"

Spilligan shook his head.

"She did not. She said that this man hadn't given his name to her, but that the Baron would know who he was."

The room fell silent for a while. Husher and Pearce mulled over the information in their minds.

"Do you recall ever getting a visit from someone strange? Someone who might have seemed out of character in the neighborhood or amongst the guests or visitors that usually called upon the Baron and Lady?" asked Lady Marmalade.

"No, nothing unusual," said Spilligan. "Though there were..."

Spilligan stopped himself mid- sentence and said no more. He gazed at the floor, or what floor he might have been able to see.

"What is it?" asked Frances.

Spilligan shook his head wearily.

"I'd really rather not. I'd rather not speak ill of my employer."

Husher smacked his hand down hard on the table. It startled everyone except for Pearce with its loud bang.

"Look here, Spilligan," said Husher in his booming voice. "You'll be right forthcoming you will or I'll make it my mission to make sure that all of your days are filled with misery."

Spilligan looked up at him, both quite terrified as well as in anger. In fact, hatred was written all over his face as plain as the sun sits in the sky.

"She was a philanderer alright? She was a loose woman and there were many men who came by to see her."

"Who?" asked Frances rather calmly.

"Several of the members of the House of Lords. I particularly remember Lord Paussage and Lord Huppington."

"I see," said Frances.

"What about Lord Loughty?" asked Husher.

Spilligan nodded.

"Yes, he's been around quite a bit," he said.

Husher grinned and looked over at Lady Marmalade. Spilligan noticed Husher's gloating look.

"I meant, Inspector," said Spilligan, "that Lord Loughty was over often, but not for Lady Marphallow. He came always to speak with the Baron."

Husher's smiled skulked off his face and he looked down at the floor and pulled at his cheeks with his mouth.

"Did the Baron know about this?" asked Frances.

"Everyone knew," he said. "Probably the whole government too."

"Did they know about each other?"

"I don't know. I'd be speculating... perhaps."

"What gives you reason to think that they might

have?" asked Frances.

"Well, about a fortnight or so ago I came upon Lady Marphallow and Lord Paussage quarreling. I thought I heard the name Huppington so I went in to see if I could offer him something to drink. He wasn't there. I apologized for the error. But it appeared that the name had come up in some sort of quarrel between the two."

Frances nodded.

"And that money that was found in your overcoat," said Pearce. "You have no idea how it got there?"

Spilligan nodded.

"No idea at all," he said.

"Was there always someone in the kitchen throughout the day on Saturday?" asked Frances.

Spilligan looked up thoughtfully for a moment.

"I can't say I remember," he said. "It was such chaos, we were all in and out of the kitchen throughout the morning."

"And why were you late?" asked Pearce, "on the morning of the Baron's murder."

Spilligan looked up sheepishly.

"I was out late with some friends," he said. "I overslept. I'm afraid it's as simple as that. Work has been stressful you see, especially of late with the arguments in the house."

Frances understood. Pearce did too, though he didn't say anything to it.

"What sort of arguments?" asked Frances.

"Well, between the Baron and the Lady as I mentioned. Also with the skulking around between the Lady and her gentlemen. She was quite adamant that we were sworn to secrecy. She didn't want a word let out to anyone."

Frances nodded.

"And then there was the argument between Lord Loughty and Lord Paussage. It ended with Lord Loughty punching Lord Paussage and storming off."

"I see. And when was that?" asked Pearce, jotting notes down in a small book.

"The 22nd I think it would have been," said Spilligan. "Let me see," and he took a moment to reflect. "Yes indeed, it was a week ago today."

Frances knew that Loughty had a bit of a temper, though he didn't seem to be a murderous man. Still, some questions would need asking.

"Well then," said Husher, getting back into the conversation. "If you didn't kill your employer, where were you between 10pm and 2am on Friday evening going into Saturday morning?"

"I was with some friends," he said. "I left the Marphallows at 10pm. Just after. Lady Marphallow was mixing a tonic for the Baron as he sat smoking a cigar on the couch he was found in the next day. I asked if they needed anything more and then I was dismissed. I was with my friends by 10:30."

"Is it usual for you to be kept until that time at night?" asked Pearce.

"No, not often. Though on that evening the Baron and Lady Marphallow had some friends over. Lord and Lady Smithwick. They had left by 9:30."

Frances knew Lord and Lady Smithwick. Quiet, good people. He was a businessman and a man not normally associated with politics. It was likely a social call and nothing more.

"And where were you with your friends?"

Spilligan looked up sheepishly again.

"Now is not the time to be holding out," said Husher threateningly.

"The Duke and Lady," said Spilligan softly.

Frances knew of it. It was a pub that often catered to homosexual men in the North of London.

"Of course you were," said Husher, "and we'll be sure to follow up on that."

Spilligan didn't say anything else. Husher looked around at Pearce and Frances as if gauging their readiness to wrap up the questioning.

"One last thing if I might, Inspector," said Frances.

Husher nodded at her.

"Did you notice anyone or anything unusual as you left the residence that Friday evening?"

"Not particularly," said Spilligan, "though now that you mention it, there were these three men in a vacant lot across the street who were dressed as laborers. I didn't think much of it at the time, but come to think of it, it seems quite odd they were there at such an hour."

Frances nodded. Pearce looked up at the Inspector. "Boyle and friends, I assume," he said.
Husher nodded.

CHAPTER FIFTEEN

Scotland Yard

FRANCES had decided to stay at Scotland Yard. They had taken a break for lunch shortly after one. Frances had gone to a local restaurant overlooking the Thames where she enjoyed fish with a side order of scalloped potatoes and green beans. It was succulent and moist and delicious. One of the best restaurants in town and it had earned its reputation honestly. The restaurant was called The Angler of Eden.

Pearce had suggested that Lady Marmalade return at two. He was sure that they would have Aidan Boyle in custody by then and she was welcome to join them for the interview. This is something she wanted to do. She had known about the Irish Republican Militia for sometime and had no sympathy for their methods, though their cause was another matter.

The rain had let up as she walked the mile or so back to Scotland Yard. The day might have been considered dreary to some, but for an autumnal day in late November it was as good as it was likely to get. As such, it had brought out many people for strolls after lunch. Though Frances didn't bump into anyone she knew.

When she arrived at the police station she notified the desk sergeant who she was and who she was meeting. Moments later, Pearce came out and escorted her back to Husher's office. The three of them sat down. Husher steepled his fingers in front of him and then leaned on them before he spoke.

"My dear Frances," he said. " This chap Aidan Boyle is quite the ruffian. He's not likely to be polite or to pay particular attention to your title. Rather, he's likely to try and rankle your feathers I should imagine. I just thought you should know. Fair warning and all."

Frances smiled at Husher. She tried to remain polite, but his mixed metaphor was awful. She wasn't sure how feathers could get rankled. Ruffled certainly, but rankled seemed odd. Nevertheless, she wasn't about to let Aidan Boyle rankle her emotions or ruffle any feathers she might not have.

"Thank you, Inspector, for your concern. I assure you, I've been in this position before, unfortunately. I have a way with the uncouth that seems to disarm their acerbic edge."

"Very well, you've been forewarned. He came in clawing and scratching."

Frances smiled at the Inspector again and nodded

politely. Pearce sat mute to her right. They all rose after Husher and Pearce led them back to the very same interview room that only a couple of hours before held Spilligan. The constable outside however, was a different man. He unlocked the door and let them all in. They sat in the same positions as they had before, and Husher stood again to Pearce's right.

Boyle was leaning in on the table when they came in, a cigarette in his left hand, his two wrists cuffed together. He had a boyish face but one that showed his age. It was freckled with a mop of red hair on top, but the crow's feet had clawed and scratched at the sides of his eyes violently, though the green eyes themselves twinkled mischievously. His left cheek was scuffed and somewhat swollen and there was a small cut above his upper lip that looked fresh, though it didn't bleed.

"So you've come to 'ave a turn then 'ay, Inspector?" said Boyle before inhaling on his cigarette.

"A turn at what."

Boyle brought up both of his hands to his upper lip and then his cheek.

"Give me a bashin' that's what," he said.

He laid his hands back down on the table in an arrow towards Frances. His cigarette stuck out between his left fingers, squashed and angry on the end.

"This is what these bobbies do, miss," he said, looking at Frances. "These fine English bobbies rough up an 'onest man, they do."

"That's terrible, just terrible," said Frances. "You ought to complain."

Boyle nodded vigorously.

"I plan on it," he said. "I will do."

"I'm sure you'll get a lot of sympathy from whomever you complain to. In these parts we're all very sympathetic to the IRM and the perpetrators of the Bloody Sunday attack."

Frances didn't know he was involved, but it was common knowledge that the IRM was involved and Aidan Boyle being one of the main foot soldiers, it would be quite an accurate assumption.

Boyle looked back at Frances and smoked his cigarette. He didn't bat an eye as she kept his eyes locked to hers.

"You a coppa' then 'ay. They puttin' female coppa's in Scotland Yard now?"

"This is Lady Marmalade, Boyle," said Husher, getting red in the face. "And you'll give her the courtesy she has earned or I will be bashing on your face."

Frances looked over at him. There had been enough violence and talk of violence in the last few days. She didn't feel like stomaching anymore, but she didn't say anything. Boyle leaned back in his chair putting his hands in his lap with the cigarette. His wiry frame gave the impression that he was not much more than skin and bones. His clothes hung on him like he was a collection of steel clothes hangers.

"Terrible business that," he said at last. "But you can un'erstand the complaints us Irish 'ave can't you, Lady?"

"It's difficult to hear the complaints when the sound of violence is crashing all around your ears," she replied.

"We're not here to talk about you Irish and your problems," said Pearce.

"No," said Boyle with a cheeky twinkle in his eye. "We 'ere for tea an' crumpet then?"

"You were found skulking around the Baron's place up on Bishops Avenue," continued Pearce.

"Me and my mates were working. A man's gotta make a livin' right?"

"At eleven at night?" asked Pearce.

Husher was getting annoyed. He was grinding his teeth like he might have been chewing on a leather bit.

"Now listen here, Boyle. I've had enough of you and your sort. We've got you on trespass, and as sure as God made little green apples I'm going to get you on that Bloody Sunday massacre. The only question is whether you want to help yourself or make it harder on yourself. Right now, my men are rounding up the rest of you ne'er do wells. In fact, I have it on good information that I'm going to find Ahearn, McClery, Payne, Nolan and maybe Clooney if I'm lucky enough."

Boyle looked over at the Inspector with a hard

stare. No longer were his Irish eyes smiling.

"You take me out of these cuffs, Inspector and I'll show you right quick 'ow a Irishman defends 'is own."

"As you wish," said Inspector Husher, and he reached into his pocket for a handcuff key and walked over to Boyle to release his handcuffs. Boyle held out his hands with a wide grin on his face and the cigarette stuck in the corner of his mouth.

"Inspector," said Frances. "If you boys would like to go about boxing each other's ears, I'd rather you did it after I'd left."

"Agreed, Inspector. Perhaps later you can offer your lesson to Boyle here," said Pearce.

Husher looked over at Frances and Pearce and his shoulders sank slightly. He backed away from Boyle and stood back on Pearce's right.

"That's a shame, Inspector, I was really 'oping to show you what for," said Boyle, grinning from ear to ear.

"Listen, Mr. Boyle," said Lady Marmalade, getting a tad annoyed at the boyish bravado in the room. "I'm a well connected woman who has the ear of many a judge. If you're willing to be helpful I'll promise to put in a good word."

Boyle stared at Frances for a while.

"An' 'ow can I trust your Ladyship?" he asked.

"Because I give you my word."

Boyle looked at her for a while.

"An English prison is no place for an Irishman," she

said. "I know what happens when young lads from the Emerald Isle get caught up in the wrong place. It's not just the other prisoners you've got to worry about it. Oh no, the guards don't much care for IRM members either."

"You drive an 'ard bargain, miss," he said, smoke curling up the side of his face like a veil. "What you want?"

"I'm primarily concerned about the murder of Baron Marphallow. I want to know why you were there and what you saw, and whether you murdered him."

Boyle took a last smoke on his cigarette and then put it out in the tin ashtray in front of him. He leaned over his forearms on the table before he began to speak.

"I'll not give up me mates," he said.

Frances shrugged.

"That's no matter, so long as they had nothing to do with the murder."

"Now listen here," said Husher, "I'd rather not give him any special concessions."

"Then I'm not speaking," said Boyle, leaning back into his chair with his hands crossed across his chest.

"I imagine good old fashioned police work will get you the men you seek, Inspector," said Frances, "and I'd really like to know what Mr. Boyle saw that evening, assuming he didn't murder the Baron."

"Alright then," said Husher, still frustrated.

Boyle leaned in again and rested his forearms on the table.

"I'd first like to understand why you were looking in on the Baron's home," said Frances.

"Well you see, miss," said Boyle, thinking that term was one of reverence for Lady Marmalade, "the Baron and some of them people like 'im aren't all that 'igh and mighty as you might think."

"We know he had money problems," said Frances, trying to get Boyle to head into deeper waters and not the shallows which had already been fished.

"Yeah, I'd 'eard he 'ad problems with money. Somethin' 'bout liking the 'orses. Well, he owns a whisky making facility."

"The Red Beagle," said Frances. "He is a part owner."

"Yes, miss, but he's been in business with us to supply the Americans with whisky. You know under the table like."

"The Americans have prohibition," said Husher.

Boyle nodded his head and grinned at the Inspector.

"That's right, and murder is illegal too, but it didn't stop the Baron from getting killed did it?"

Boyle turned back towards Frances.

"The Americans pay a lot of money for what they like and what they want," he continued.

"How much?" asked Frances.

"Well, it's all sold in cases yeah. And there's twelve bot'ls to a case. We pay the Baron per case at one 'undred pounds per case."

"That's an outrageous sum," said Husher, "I don't believe it for minute."

"Don't matter if you don't believe it. I'm just tellin' you 'ow it 'appens. Our lads in New York get it from us for two 'undred. What they sell it for is up to them."

"I can believe it, Inspector," said Lady Marmalade. "That works out to at least sixteen pounds a bottle. And I'm assuming the Americans are paying for shipping?"

Frances looked at Boyle, and he nodded.

"So at least eighteen pounds to get it there. Who knows how much Boyle's friends in America are selling it for, but certainly not less than three hundred pounds a case."

"I reckon at least that, if they're smart," interjected Boyle.

"I've heard that in some of the Mafia controlled speakeasies a shot of Irish whisky will go for five or six dollars."

"You must be joking?" said the Inspector incredulously.

"Not at all," said Frances. "Irish whisky is prized over Scottish, and it's unavailable except on the black market, and who knows how much is being smuggled in."

"We're the biggest. That I know for a fact," said Boyle.

Frances nodded at Boyle and then looked back over at the Inspector.

"There you go, Inspector. Most Americans who are drinking and that is most Americans overall, are drinking what they call moonshine. Cheap awful stuff so I'm told. But those who can afford it will pay a premium for the real stuff. French wine when it can be had I've heard will go for ten or twenty pounds, and that's not for anything fancy."

Husher frowned and looked over at Pearce.

"You know about this?" he asked.

"I've heard rumors," said Pearce. "Not surprising though. Making something illegal doesn't make it disappear, in fact it often encourages its illicit use. However, prohibition has just started. We're going to have our hands full with this sort of thing the longer it goes on."

Husher didn't say anything.

"As I understand it," said Frances, "prohibition started at the beginning of the year in January sometime."

"I see," said Pearce.

Lady Marmalade looked over at Boyle.

"How long have you been providing liquor?"

"Since the spring miss. But we've only been with the Baron since July."

"And getting round to the main thrust of my question. Why were you watching Baron Marphallow's home?"

Boyle leaned back and smiled coyly.

"You see, we needed to talk to 'im about some of the

improprieties in our business dealings."

"Such as?"

"He was trying to stiff us."

"How was he doing that?"

"He was diluting the whisky. He was selling us twelve bot'ls of whisky but only giving us ten. He was diluting ten bot'ls into twelve you see."

"I see. So you were just going to talk to him then, is that what I'm to understand?"

Boyle smiled mischievously, and nodded his head.

"Yes, miss, exactly that. We just wanted to 'ave a friendly conversation with 'im like."

"Bollocks," said Husher. "You murdered a bunch of men in cold blood, not a month ago and you expect us to believe that you were just going to have a polite conversation with the Baron."

Boyle nodded at the Inspector.

"Exactly like that, yes, sir. I'm not a violent man."

Pearce shook his head slowly.

"More likely you were beaten to the murder. Did you get to have this talk with the Baron?"

"No we didn't, constable. We was just s'posed to 'ave a look and see when a good time to talk with the Baron might be."

"So what did you see?" asked Pearce.

"We saw a well dressed couple leave around nine thirty in the evening. They seemed to be friends of the Baron's. He came out to wave goodbye. Him and 'is missus. They were dressed real fine."

"What else?" asked Pearce.

"Then I reckon I saw the butler leave. Must 'ave been around ten that night."

"How did you know he was the butler?" asked Frances.

"He was dressed like one. He saw us, but I gave 'im a look as to suggest he'd be better off minding his own business."

"And from ten until eleven, what did you see?" asked Husher.

"Saw this tall chap come by. He looked like a Lord."

"How would you describe him?" asked Husher.

"He was a tall, thin man," said Boyle. "Very tall he was. Had on a hat, and he walked up to the Baron's place but he didn't go in. He turned before he reached the door."

Husher looked at Lady Marmalade.

"Doesn't sound like Paussage or Huppington," he said.

Frances nodded.

"I'll talk to Loughty about it," was all she said.

Husher nodded.

"What time was that?" he said turning to look at Boyle.

"Before ten thirty. Maybe ten fifteen or ten twenty. We wasn't paying close attention to time you understand."

"Anything else?" asked Husher.

"Yeah, one other thing, Inspector," said Boyle, "just

before we was requested to leave by your man we saw another fellow walk up to the 'ouse. Also dressed real nice like. That must 'ave been close to eleven."

"And how would you describe this other man?" asked Lady Marmalade.

"Well fed. I'd say he was two or maybe three of me. A big fat man, short too with a bald head. Couldn't get a real good look, but he done walked up and the lady of the 'ouse she lets 'im in, and pops her nose out to take a look see. What for I 'ave no idea."

"You see him before?" asked Pearce.

"No I 'aven't, constable. I'm not often over on this side of the shore you know."

Pearce looked at Lady Marmalade.

"Huppington or Paussage?" he asked her.

"Sounds more like Paussage," said Frances.

Pearce nodded.

"We might have our man," he said, looking from Lady Marmalade to Husher.

Husher grunted something that sounded like agreement.

"I'm free to go then right, Inspector?"

Husher looked at him and shook his head slowly.

"You taking to clowning around now are you, Boyle? Do I look like the circus to you?"

Boyle didn't say anything, he just smiled at the Inspector.

"You're in here for the long haul mate. As soon as we get some of those witnesses from Dublin, your days of strolling free are gone, Boyle."

Husher stood up, and then Pearce and lastly Frances. Boyle leaned in and reached out for Lady Marmalade but he couldn't reach her. He looked up at her earnestly.

"You promised, miss," he said. "You promised you'd put in a good word."

Boyle frowned at her and Lady Marmalade stopped and looked down at him.

"And I will," she said, and the three of them left the room.

"I hope you're not really hoping to put in a good word for that coldblooded murderer?" asked Pearce.

Frances smiled at him.

"I am a woman of my word constable. And I will tell the judge how helpful he was in this particular case. But whichever judge it is will understand full well that I require no compensation for Boyle's help from him or anyone else for that matter. He will receive the punishment that he rightly deserves."

Pearce nodded slowly, and slowly a grin spread across his face. He understood.

"Good," he said. "Very good."

"I've got some paperwork to do," said Husher. "I need a warrant to compel Lord Paussage to speak with us."

Frances turned towards the Inspector before he left.

"I can get you what you need, Inspector. I'll have a

confession out of him before the end of the week if he's the one who did it."

"I'd say it certainly looks like it," said Husher. "I'll wait then to hear from you."

Husher was about to leave again but Frances put her hand on his forearm to stop him.

"If you don't mind, Inspector, I'd rather like to talk with Lord Loughty in a more comfortable setting before you bring him in here for questioning, if you'll permit."

"So long as you include me," said Husher.

"Of course."

Husher left and Pearce and Lady Marmalade stood outside the room where Boyle fidgeted inside like a fish out of water.

"What do you think of this Boyle character and his involvement in the case?" she asked Pearce.

"I don't think he did it. Though if Paussage hadn't, I've a feeling that the Baron would have seen a bad end regardless."

"That's what I fear. How easily men commit these violent matters over such trifling issues."

Frances looked at down at her hands which were clasped in front of her and holding her handbag.

"Quite," said Pearce, looking at her for a moment. "Can I take you home now?"

Frances looked up at him.

"Yes, thank you."

And with that she followed him out of the building

and into the fuzzy day. At least that's what it felt like to her. A fuzzy, unkempt day that nuzzled at you like an undisciplined dog or else rained on you when it couldn't make up its mind.

By the time Frances got home, it was pouring. Quite an unusual heavy rain that was quite uncommon for the tail end of autumn, and it made her think of the sad, awkward endings to men's lives having lived so desperately incongruently with even a basic morality.

CHAPTER SIXTEEN

Loughty Residence

THE following morning had opened the day to a bright sun. It seemed all was forgiven. The only knowledge of the rain from the day before was the still damp grass and the little blisters of it left over on the leaves that had not been torn from limbs by the careless fingers of autumn.

Lord Loughty had made himself available to Lady Marmalade this very afternoon. He didn't live far from the Baron, and as much as he vehemently disagreed with the man's politics, he had found him to be an astute debater and passionate politician. Eric was going to take her to his home for three. He was offering sandwiches and tea, and if the day kept to its promise of sunny skies, it would be a tea for the history books.

Lady Marmalade waited for Eric to bring the car round. He had gone into the office for the morning but had come home for a lunch at one. He pulled the car out front and came back inside.

"It's absolutely wonderful out there, darling," he said, grinning from ear to ear.

"Really? It looks lovely, but is it actually warm?"

"I'd say so. Might even be warm enough to have tea out on the lawn if Larmer's up for it. It must be close to fifteen degrees. A perfect spring day in the dying days of autumn."

"So I don't need much of a coat then."

"I'd take something just to be sure, but not your winter jacket."

Alfred had joined them in the hallway and he helped Lady Marmalade get her autumnal jacket out of the closet. It was a double lined chocolate brown jacket that was knee length. She put on matching brown gloves. Underneath she wore a calf length cream colored skirt with an off white blouse underneath a woolen cream colored Aran pullover with cable pattern. Eric wore a dark grey three piece suit with patent leather shoes and black driving gloves.

"Dinner for when you get back?" asked Alfred.

Frances turned to look at him.

"Not sure how long we'll be," said Frances. "Perhaps not earlier than seven."

"Certainly, my Lady," said Alfred.

"I'll send Ginny off to the butcher just before he closes. It's lamb chops tonight."

"Sounds jolly good," said Eric. "Let's be off, dear, we

don't want to be late."

Eric led Frances out the front door and into the car. Alfred closed the door behind them and went back to his chores.

"I can't decide if the Baron's murder is going to help the IRM or hurt them," he said once they were well on their way.

"It shouldn't have anything to do with it," said Frances.

"Why not?" he asked.

"Because they weren't involved in his death."

"I thought you said they would've been if he hadn't have been murdered before they had a chance to get to him."

"Yes, darling, but that's not the point. They didn't do it, so they can't be responsible for something they didn't do."

"Surely this bootlegging business is going to come back on them."

"It will, but they're not known as a charity. I think the public will be hardly surprised to learn that the IRM is in yet more illegal activities. If anything, I should think His Majesty's Government is going to have some explaining to do. I'd say it's given them a black eye."

"That the Baron was murdered."

"No, dear, that their beloved Woolsack was involved with the IRM in providing illegal liquor to the Americans from his own distillery."

"Yes, I can see how that's going to make things awkward for them."

"I think making it awkward is putting it mildly. David George has a lot of explaining to do. I should think the next election will not go to the Liberals but likely the Conservatives."

"I thought you liked George?" asked Eric.

"As far as a politician goes, I do rather like him. But my personal feelings shan't hamper my professional opinions."

Frances looked at Eric out of the corner of her eye with a wry smile on her face. Eric looked over at her and let out a hearty laugh.

"So he won't get your vote then, will he?" asked Eric.

"That remains to be seen, my dear. I'll have to see if he still runs and who's running against him."

They drove in silence for the rest of the way. They arrived with ten minutes to spare, and Lady Marmalade didn't see any police cars parked outside the large residence on Bishops Avenue.

"Looks like we beat Pearce and Husher," she said.

"Good," replied Eric.

"Yes, it is very good. I want to have a chat with Larmer before the police get here. That Inspector Husher can be a little bullheaded sometimes and I fear he just puts people's hackles up."

Eric helped Frances out of the car.

"You attract more bees with sweet honey rather

than vinegar, don't you, darling."

Frances nodded, taking Eric's hand as he got out of the car. They walked up the front walkway and to the large wooden door. Eric wrapped the door with the large brass door knocker looking like a lion's head.

Larmer opened the door to them personally. He was a tall and distinguished looking Irishman. Frances liked him a lot, though they didn't visit with him as often as she would have liked. He was a man in his early forties and had never been married. There was much speculation about that, but nothing that could be proved. Frances believed, and rightly so, that he was just disinterested.

"Thank you for having us," said Lady Marmalade.

"Not at all," said Loughty, "it is always a treat to have the Marmalades over for any reason. Though a happier reason is always preferred."

"Isn't it just," agreed Eric, and then added. "What a glorious day we're having."

"Too right. If you're both up for it, I though we should dine outside on the lawn. There isn't very much wind and it's right in the sun."

"Frances and I were just talking about that on the way here," said Eric.

"Good, good," said Loughty, leading them through the house and into the backyard which was an oasis of tranquility. Hedges and trees and gardens for plants were abundant. The grass which was not as green as it would be in the spring and summer was still lush and soft through the feet. They sat down and Frances did find it quite warm and pleasant to be outside at this time of year.

A younger man, perhaps in his early to mid-thirties came up to Loughty. He was clearly a butler by the way he was dressed, and Frances had met him several times before.

"Tea and sandwiches, my Lord?" he asked Loughty.

"Wonderful, and do please keep an eye out for the police. I'm expecting a constable and an inspector at the very least. Show them in and bring them outside to join us when they arrive."

Loughty's butler bowed himself away.

"A wonderful garden you have, Larm," said Frances, looking around at the spacious, rolling grounds. Eric nodded. Loughty brought it all in with a sweeping gaze.

"Thank you, Fran," he said. "It brings me great peace and calm whenever I'm out here. Especially when times are difficult as they have been lately. I often have my best thoughts in this garden. Weather permitting of course."

"It's quite a bit larger than our garden, wouldn't you say, darling?" asked Frances, turning to look at her husband. Eric nodded.

"Quite," he said.

Loughty turned to look at the both of them.

"Aha, but this is my kingdom, my castle if you will. I don't have estates dotted around the countryside," he said, grinning at both of them.

Frances smiled back.

"But it is quite lovely," she said.

"It is. It is my greatest joy. I don't know if you knew this, but I like to spend quite a bit of time tending to the gardens myself."

"But you do employ a groundskeeper as I recall," said Eric.

"Oh yes, but I love to get my hands into the soil. Something primal and peaceful about it, to remember where one comes from," said Loughty. "Remember, man, thou art dust and to dust thou shall return."

He smiled at them and looked away at the gardens again. After a pause he spoke.

"Dreadful business what happened to my neighbor, the Baron."

The Baron wasn't strictly Loughty's neighbor, he was several houses away, but those who lived on the Bishops Avenue thought of each other as neighbors regardless of the distance between each.

Neither Eric nor Frances said anything to that.

"Though I confess to not liking the man, one never wishes such calamity upon one's enemies."

"You didn't really consider him an enemy, did you?" asked Frances.

Loughty turned to Frances and smiled at her.

"Not in that sense, no. But if you'd asked me a week ago, I would have acknowledged that we were political enemies certainly. But then again, I could say the same thing about all of Lloyd George's men."

The butler came out with the housekeeper and laid silver trays of assorted sandwiches and plates and knives on the table in the middle of them. There was a also a silver teapot on another silver tray with a silver bowl of sugar and a silver carafe of milk and one of cream.

"I know you prefer cream with your tea," said Loughty looking at the silver tray carrying the tea and accessories.

"You're very kind," replied Frances.

"Anything else, my Lord?" asked the butler.

"Just keep an eye out for the police, if you will," said Loughty.

The butler and housekeeper left them.

"I can't believe our good luck with the weather today. Quite peculiar," said Eric. "Though I'll take it."

"It's the world's aching urge for spring," said Loughty.

Frances smiled.

"I fear she'll ache a while longer," she said. "We haven't even entered winter yet."

"The winter of discontent," said Loughty. "Speaking of which, how is business Eric?"

"Across the board, it's not as good as one would hope. We've had to let go quite a few good men. A real shame."

"It actually pains him," said Frances. "He's not quite the cutthroat businessman he pretends to be."

"And never was he," added Loughty. "A princely man with a decent soul. That's the sort we need to build our economy back to what it once was."

"You're very kind," said Eric.

"Nevertheless," said Loughty, "I'm sorry to hear of the difficulties. The war has certainly cast its long shadow into this our future."

Eric nodded.

"Though British ingenuity, labor and downright bullheadedness will get us back on the right path."

"It most certainly will," said Larmer.

"Of course," said Eric, "across the pond, our American friends are seeing great and robust growth."

"But how stable will it be?" asked Loughty.

"That remains to be seen," said Eric.

"Can I pour tea?" asked Loughty.

He poured tea for Frances and Eric and Frances helped herself to cream and sugar. Eric took his black as usual as there were no lemons available. Frances took a cucumber sandwich. Eric waited.

"Thank God for small mercies," said Frances, taking a sip of tea.

"Indeed. We are fortunate. A cup of tea melts away all the world's troubles doesn't it, my dear?" said Eric.

"I'll drink to that," said Loughty. "You'll forgive me. I presumed that sandwiches would be quite alright, though I can get Margaret to bake up some scones if you'd prefer."

"Nonsense," said Frances. "Sandwiches are perfectly fine and more than that, they're delicious."

Loughty smiled.

"Glad to hear it."

Behind them they heard some commotion. They all peered round and saw Husher and Pearce being led across the lawn towards them by the butler. Both men wore grey raincoats and hats. The three of them stood up.

"Inspector Husher," said Husher as he introduced himself to Loughty and shook hands with him. He shook hands with Lord Marmalade though he already knew him and he nodded at Frances in turn. He turned towards Pearce.

"This is Constable Pearce," said Husher, "he's helping me with the case."

Pearce shook hands with the two men and nodded at Frances.

"Quite a young man to be in homicide," said Loughty.

Pearce nodded.

"The youngest they've had," he said.

Loughty waved at the two spare chairs that were available.

"Please take a seat," he said.

Pearce and Husher walked over to the chairs which were opposite Eric and Frances and to Loughty's left. They all waited until Frances had sat down before they sat themselves.

"Can I offer you some tea and sandwiches?" asked Loughty.

Husher shook his head.

"No, thank you," he said.

"I'd love some," said Pearce.

Loughty poured a cup of tea for Pearce. Pearce added milk and sugar to it. He also helped himself to a couple of cucumber sandwiches which were cut into triangular quarters.

"You know why we're here," said Husher. "A very grave crime has been committed and we have new information that we'd like to have cleared up by you, if you don't mind."

Husher's mannerism might have been gruff, but he was still professional and quite politically astute. Loughty might be a crossbencher but you never knew when he might make it to the government's side, and a police officer like Husher knew that any friends he could make or keep in politics were allies earned.

Loughty nodded while reaching for a plate upon which he put two sandwich quarters on it. He poured himself some tea and looked over at his butler. The butler came up and took the teapot away to refill.

"Terribly sad what happened to my peer," said Loughty. "I'd like to help as best I can."

"We've had a chance to speak with a few more witnesses, including staff at the Marphallow residence," continued Husher.

Pearce looked on, taking a bite of his sandwich. He

enjoyed being the constable, the assistant to the Inspector. He got to observe and clear his thoughts.

"Yes, I have heard that the butler was caught stealing some money from them," said Loughty.

Husher didn't answer that.

"Which brings me to my first question. Did you know of any money problems that the Baron and his wife might have been experiencing?"

Loughty took a moment to chew on his sandwich before he spoke. Then he shook his head slowly.

"No, I'm afraid not..." he paused for a while before continuing. "Though there were rumors, of course, about the Baron's gambling and Lady Marphallow's spendthrift ways."

"But nothing that you were intimately aware of?" asked Husher.

Larmer shook his head, put his plate of sandwiches down, which still held one quarter and about a mouthful of the second quarter left. He picked up his saucer and teacup and took a sip of it. He took his tea black. The butler came back and put a fresh pot of tea back down on the silver tray and discreetly moved out of hearing distance.

"You must understand, Inspector," said Loughty, "I was not on the government's bench and nor was I close to any of them. All I know about the Baron's financial matters are nothing more than rumors or speculation. Though of course where there's smoke there is often a fire."

Husher nodded.

"I have first hand knowledge of the Baron's monetary troubles," said Eric. "His wife spent extravagantly and he had a weakness for the horses. I'm not often at the races but whenever I go, the Baron is there in the Prince's box and always spending large sums, and generally losing them. It doesn't surprise me to learn that he was engaged in shady dealings with the IRM."

Husher looked at Eric without emotion. Loughty turned towards Eric.

"You don't say, our own Woolsack in league with the devil, eh?"

Loughty was more amused than angry.

"Quite," said Eric. "Selling his whisky to the Americans, we understand, with the help of the IRM."

"Not surprising nothing good came of it," said Loughty.

"Lady Marmalade doesn't seem to think they had anything to do with it," said Husher.

Loughty looked over at her. Frances smiled at him.

"Not that I don't think they didn't want to bring him injury, I just believe they didn't have the chance."

Loughty nodded and sipped tea. Pearce started on his second sandwich. Frances sipped her tea and then reached for her sandwich.

"Do you know of any dealings he might have had with the IRM, Lord Loughty?" asked Husher.

Loughty shook his head.

Jason Blacker

"No I don't, Inspector. This comes as a surprise to me. All my dealings with him were strictly professional and related to politics. Though now that I hear about this, it is interesting to note how he didn't take as hard a line on the IRM as some of his colleagues did. Specifically Lord Paussage."

"Speaking of which," said Husher. "I understand that you met with Lord Paussage and the Baron at the Baron's home on the Monday the 22nd."

"That is correct," said Loughty.

"Can you tell me what happened on that evening?" asked Husher.

"Well, we discussed politics as usual. I lost my temper and left."

"I'd prefer a little more detail, Lord Loughty, if you don't mind," said Husher.

"We were discussing the Bloody Sunday attacks," said Loughty. "As you might know from the papers, the government is adamant that the only approach is to take a hard line with the IRM and perhaps even Ceann Daoine."

Husher nodded, not saying anything. He preferred to stay out of politics, though being a government man and perhaps even more so a man of the law he was sympathetic to taking a hard line with all terrorists.

"I went over to try and convince them that a more diplomatic approach was the preferred method. I advised them that Ceann Daoine had clearly distanced themselves from the more presently militant IRM. Paussage wouldn't hear of it. Marphallow on the other hand was more sympathetic to hearing me out, though I don't think he was moved by my plea for reason."

"I see," said Husher, still staying out of the politics. "And I assume then, that it went from bad to worse?"

Loughty nodded and took a sip of tea. Pearce finished his second quarter of sandwich and put his plate down. He was considering taking another couple of quarters but thought it might be considered rude.

"Please have as much as you want," said Loughty, seeing Pearce's indecision.

"That's very kind," said Pearce as he took two more quarters. Loughty smiled, wondering if the police didn't paid enough for lunchtime meals. And in fact, Pearce had not had the time today to get a lunch. Frances and Eric sipped on their tea and cradled their saucers in their laps, enjoying the surroundings, the warm weather, and keeping an ear to the conversation.

"To get back to your question, Inspector, yes, things went from bad to worse. Lord Paussage is a difficult man to like. Well, especially from this side of the bench..."

"He's a difficult man to like whatever side of the bench you're on," said Eric, grinning.

Loughty looked over at him and smiled.

"I was trying to be more polite," he said. He turned back to face Husher. "He has a way of getting under one's skin. He makes snide comments and is definitely rude."

"You'll forgive me for being forthright, Lord Loughty," said Husher, "but under these circumstances we need to get to the bottom of this crime."

Loughty nodded at him, and paused to sip tea.

"It has come to my attention that you struck Lord Paussage and threatened Baron Marphallow. Is that true?"

Loughty nodded.

"The former is true, the latter I think is a reach."

"Can you explain?"

"Well, Inspector, I sometimes forget that politics is not a combative sport. I boxed for my varsity team, and sometimes that gets the better of me."

"I see."

"I'm joking, Inspector. This is what happened. It started off unpleasantly. Paussage sometimes thinks he knows everything. We were drinking Scottish whisky, or as I like to call it, the Scotsman's tea. Paussage, who I don't believe is even Scottish, was bragging about Scottish whisky being the finest and the first. On both accounts he's wrong."

"I didn't realize that," said Pearce, finally getting into the conversation. "I thought the Scottish invented whisky."

Loughty shook his head slowly and sadly.

"No, I'm afraid not, that's what they'll have you believe and that myth has somehow taken hold."

Eric nodded.

"The Irish were first," he said, "and I'd agree with Larmer that they make the best whisky as a whole too."

"You have very fine taste, my Lord," said Larmer raising his teacup to Eric with a twinkle in his eye.

"No matter," said Pearce, "I've always preferred Irish whisky over Scottish. Just a personal preference."

"And you, sir," said Loughty, raising his teacup to Pearce, "are also a man of refined tastes."

Pearce raised his cup to Loughty and nodded at him.

"And I prefer neither," said Frances. "I'll stick to my gin and tonics."

"Another excellent choice, my Lady," said Loughty, "gin as you might know is also an Irish invention."

Loughty was having a hard time keeping his impishness at bay.

"Now I know you're putting me on," said Frances. "It was invented by the Dutch and gave us the term Dutch Courage."

"Not only are you wonderful company, Frances, but you are a natural scholar," said Loughty.

Husher was getting a bit bored.

"Ahem," he said. "If we can get back to the question

at hand."

"Certainly," said Loughty. He drained his teacup and put it down on the table.

"It started off with an argument about whisky. Then it devolved into an argument over how best to proceed with the Bloody Sunday massacre."

Husher nodded.

"Paussage thrust a few more barbs my way. He suggested that His Majesty's Government knew what was best for the Irish. This came about because I enlightened him about the Irish people having voted for Ceann Daoine in the first place, and that if they wanted to secede they should be allowed to."

"And I quite agree," said Frances, looking over at Loughty. Loughty nodded and offered a small smile.

"Before things could get worse between us, Lady Marphallow came down and bid us all a good night."

Husher nodded. Pearce finished up his third quarter of the cucumber sandwiches. Frances put her now empty teacup down, which at this point joined her husband's. She nibbled at a sandwich.

"Then we continued our debate over the best course of action to take regarding the events previously discussed. At this point Paussage called the Irish people an uncivilized and uncultured race and then he used a racial slur pointed at me, at which time I went up and hit him on the nose. Quite to his surprise I might add."

Loughty smiled at the memory.

"And if I can offer any insight, Inspector," said Eric, "I am sure that there could be no one more deserving of Loughty's wrath than Paussage."

"That's all very well," said Husher, "but in a civilized country, and I believe we like to consider ourselves civilized, we do not stoop to violence in order to solve our problems."

"You'd think so," said Frances, "and yet His Majesty's Government makes great use of it on a daily basis in our schools and prisons."

None of the men wanted to get anywhere near that, so the table fell silent. Frances finished up her cucumber sandwich.

"Has Lord Paussage complained to the police Inspector?" asked Loughty. "Does he wish me brought before the courts and charged with wounding his massive ego?"

Husher didn't say anything.

"You've answered the first part of my question Lord Loughty, what about the second part?" asked the Inspector.

"I forget, can you remind me?"

"You threatened the Baron with his life, so we've been led to believe."

"Oh yes, that nonsense. It wasn't like that at all. I told him that refusing to sit down and discuss the Irish difficulties with the Irish people or their elected representatives in Ceann Daoine would be the death of him. It seems like I was quite prescient. In any event, I was quite hot under the collar and I certainly didn't threaten himself personally."

"I see," said the Inspector.

"No," said Loughty, getting strident, "I don't think you do. You have no idea the difficult task it is to work in government. More than that, I felt I was invited over under false pretenses. I'm not sure what they were playing at, but it was certainly not to discuss the problems with an open mind. In any event, I understand that you don't think the Irish Republican Militia had anything to do with the Baron's murder, so how could my threat carry any weight."

Husher looked over at Loughty.

"That is correct, though not because they didn't want to. We believe they didn't have the chance. And this brings me to my next point, and why your threat is being taken seriously."

"Then let's get on with it, Inspector," said Loughty.

"I don't think the Inspector is accusing you, Larm," said Frances, trying to calm Loughty down, "but you might have valuable information that could help us catch the murderer."

Loughty looked over at Frances for a moment.

"Fair enough," he said. "Alright, Inspector, let's get to brass tacks."

"We caught a few witnesses on the night of the Baron's murder. They were known IRM members. They said you went back to the Baron's home the night of his murder."

Husher, who had been jotting notes in a small notebook all this time flipped back several pages.

"They put you at the Baron's home at around ten fifteen to ten thirty."

Loughty looked at the Inspector steadily for a moment.

"So you're suggesting that I went back that night... what night was that again?"

"Friday evening the 26th," offered Lady Marmalade.

"Right," continued Loughty, "so I went back a few days after our disagreement to kill the man?"

"That is not what I said," said Husher, also getting worked up. "I have come here, to your home, in goodwill and in recognition of your station and title. If it would make you more comfortable, we can continue this conversation down at the station."

Husher was not one to be pushed around. He stared down Loughty, and even though Loughty was a Lord and part of the government, he wasn't on the government's bench and he wasn't about to intimidate the Inspector in charge of homicide at Scotland Yard.

"Fair enough," said Loughty. "I didn't murder the Baron and you'd know that if your witnesses were telling the truth. Yes, I went to the Baron's home that Friday evening, but I didn't go into his home."

"Why not?" asked Husher.

"I thought it was too late."

"And why had you decided to attend at his

residence again?"

"I had been thinking of our previous conversation on that Monday evening of which we just spoke. I had gone to apologize. Now, I wish I had gone in and done that very thing."

Pearce finished eating his sandwiches. He didn't believe that Loughty had anything to do with the murder, nor did he think that anything would come of asking him about it. But he was pleased with the sandwiches and he enjoyed a cup of tea on the rolling lawn of one of England's richest Lords.

"Life is too short," said Loughty, "if this doesn't drive home that point then nothing will. Baron Marphallow might have been my political nemesis but he was not an evil man, and I now regret not having had the chance to apologize in person. These things cannot be taken back."

Frances nodded.

"But you shouldn't beat yourself up about it, Larm. These things are done, and one can only move forward with a more gracious heart. Your intention was honorable, I'm sure the Baron would have known that."

Loughty smiled at Frances and nodded.

"Is there anything else, Inspector?" he asked.

Husher looked up from his notebook, and nodded.

"Did you happen to see anyone else in that neighborhood who looked out of sorts?"

"No, no one out of sorts, but I did think I saw

Paussage heading that way."

"Go on."

"Well, I got home at around ten forty five after walking around for a bit after I'd gone up to see the Baron. I still had a lot of thinking to do. I still wanted to offer my apologies, but I wanted to do it in a private manner. I was thinking I would attend the next morning. In any event we know how that turned out."

Husher nodded at Loughty to continue.

"Well, I went into my smoking room which is at the front of the house here. It overlooks the main street. I sat down and put on my smoking jacket. I poured a good Irish whisky and packed my pipe. Shortly before eleven I should think it was. The clock chimed not long after, I noticed Paussage drive past in the direction of the Baron's."

"You are certain it was him?"

Loughty nodded.

"His silver Silver Ghost with a gold Emily is quite unmistakable. The man has gauche sensibilities."

"Emily?" asked Husher.

"The Spirit of Ecstasy," offered Lady Marmalade. "Emily, or the Spirit of Ecstasy is the small female sculpture or ornament on the bonnet of the Rolls Royce."

Husher nodded. "I see."

"Paussage had a gold one especially made for his Silver Ghost," added Loughty.

Husher nodded.

"So you are certain it was him?"

"As certain as I could be." It was dark of course, but even under the stingy street lamps I could make out his squat profile in the driver's seat."

"Very good," said Husher. He turned to look at Pearce. "Anything you might want to ask?"

Pearce shook his head.

"I don't think so, Inspector, seems we have our man. We just need to prove it."

Loughty looked at the two policemen. Eric stretched his long legs out in front of him. The sun was warm on his legs and his torso through his cardigan vest.

"That will be all," said Husher as he stood up. Pearce stood with him. They shook hands with everyone and started to leave.

"Inspector," said Frances.

Husher and Pearce turned around and Frances walked a few steps to catch up with them.

"The Government has closed for a few days. Before we get to Edith, perhaps you would care to join me at the House of Lords tomorrow at say ten o'clock?"

"What for?" asked Pearce.

"I'd like to take a look through Paussage's office to see if there is anything that might help bring further evidence to light."

Husher nodded.

"Very good, sounds like a good idea indeed."

"I'm not hopeful," she said, "but one must do one's

due diligence. I fear this was a crime of passion and as such I doubt much planning took place with it."

"So you think it might be more difficult to get a confession?" asked Pearce.

Frances shook her head.

"No, I shouldn't think so, the housekeeper will be easily led into confessing, and from there I don't think it's a reach to get Paussage to confess either."

Pearce nodded.

"Nevertheless, it'll be more helpful if we can find some evidence to use just in case. Though perhaps that won't be possible."

"See you then," said Pearce as he walked off with the Inspector.

Frances went back and sat down with Loughty and Eric. Loughty was just pouring more tea. He offered some to Frances and she accepted, pushing her cup towards him.

"Nasty business, this police business," said Loughty. "I don't envy them their jobs. Seems they make enemies wherever they go."

Frances nodded and added cream and sugar to her teacup. Eric sipped on his black tea.

"It is indeed."

"I can't imagine how you do it, Fran," continued Loughty. "Dealing with all of man's inhumanity towards man."

Frances brought her teacup to her lip and sipped on it, testing the creaminess and sweetness.

"She's very good at it, Larm," said Eric. "I think that's part of the problem."

Frances nodded.

"E's right," she said. "I sort of fell into it and I can't get out... Or should I say, I don't want to get out."

"Why not?" asked Loughty.

"Because I'm good a it, and I hate seeing justice going unserved. If I can help bring the light of justice into dark corners, I'll continue on with it."

Loughty sipped tea.

"It's very admirable. Careful it doesn't steal your soul," he said.

Frances smiled at him.

"I guard it with my life," she said.

"So you think you know who did it? You think it was Paussage?" asked Loughty.

"I am certain. Especially now that you saw him heading towards the Baron's residence."

"But I never saw him enter the residence that fateful night."

"And you wouldn't have, you were home. But where else could he have gone?"

"Perhaps he was out for an evening drive," offered Loughty.

"Not likely, besides the Baron and you, I don't believe he knows many other peers or friends on Bishops Avenue. He also lives closer to me, so why is he up here driving around at such a godforsaken hour."

Loughty nodded.

"You have a point."

"By the end of the week, I hope to have him in custody," she said.

"It's awful to think of this happening so close to home," said Eric. "I know both these men quite well. Paussage might have been a hotheaded imbecile but I never fancied him for a murderer."

"People are often not what they seem," said Frances. "And as much as we like to cloth ourselves in Queen's English and civilized behavior, we are nothing more than hairless thinking apes, and as such we need to remain ever vigilant over our baser animal natures."

Larmer and Eric nodded in agreement.

"Too true," said Loughty, and he looked out into his garden, thinking about the apes in Borneo he had seen in the forests there swinging from tree to tree and occasionally swatting each other.

CHAPTER SEVENTEEN

House of Lords

THE Palace of Westminster, and indeed the Houses of Parliament jutted up against the Thames like old dragon teeth. At least that's what Lady Marmalade thought of as she came up to the building having been driven by Alfred. He dropped her off at the corner and she walked towards the entrance. It was quiet around the parliament buildings. In respect of the Baron's death, both Houses had been closed for the first part of this week. They would reopen tomorrow.

Frances entered by way of St. Stephens' Hall and then turned right at the Central Hall and headed down Peers Corridor towards the Peers Lobby past which lay the House of Lords which was opposite the House of Commons. Frances had no difficulty finding her way around here as she had been here many times before. One of few women who had the privilege. Sadly though, no women were allowed in the House of Lords, which if she had her way would be changed immediately. But time was a rigid old man who didn't bend easily towards equality and justice.

Frances walked into the House of Lords as if she were a life peer about to take her seat. Indeed, there was no one to stop her, and she had been invited in before. Wives of the peers were allowed to visit but weren't allowed to sit. Sit in the political sense. Nevertheless, Frances, feeling somewhat cheeky went straight to the Woolsack's bench and took a seat, looking around and taking in the opulent and at the same time majestic cathedral-like atmosphere of this House.

She imagined she'd have to wait a bit for the Inspector and the Constable to arrive. The Palace of Westminster, indeed, the whole of the Houses of Parliament was a bit of a maze to the uninitiated, and she didn't imagine much police business took place here. Certainly not murder investigations. It was just a few minutes before ten.

Frances knew where the Lord Chancellor's or Woolsack's offices were. And by offices, she meant the plural. The Lord Chancellor had his own room and a separate room for his officers. They were directly west of her. They were the Old Palace Yard also known as the site of executions where Sir Walter Raleigh and Guy Fawkes amongst others of the Gunpowder Plot were executed. As was James Hamilton the 1st Duke of Hamilton after losing the Battle of Preston. But that was a long time ago, now only remembered by the history books and the likes of Lady Marmalade who felt to study history was indeed to look into the heart of the future.

Frances had a soft spot for Guy Fawkes who was executed several years earlier than James Hamilton. Their blood perhaps still clinging to the soil that lay underneath the hard ground outside in the Old Palace Yard. Being a Catholic herself she was sympathetic to the Catholic cause of trying to dethrone an unsympathetic king, King James I of England. However, she by no means supported the violent means by which they attempted to achieve their ends.

Nevertheless, the Gunpowder Plot was over 300 years ago. And yet it felt very recent. Perhaps because of the current violence committed by the Catholic IRM, just a couple of weeks before. Indeed, looking back into history did seem to give one a chance to read about the heart of the future.

From the Lord Chancellor's office, if Lady Marmalade remembered correctly, you could crane your head and look out to your right, facing north and you could see the statue of Richard the Lionheart. It is an equestrian statue with King Richard I in a mail shirt with his hand held high in victory grasping a sword. History was written by victors. Perhaps if the Gunpowder Plot had been successful you might instead see a statue of Sir Walter Raleigh or perhaps even Guy Fawkes where Richard coeur de lion now stood proudly.

Frances heard footsteps and she looked down the hall and away from the ornate gold ceiling which had captured her attention. Inspector Husher and Constable Pearce walked towards her with confidence, their raincoats billowing out the sides from the air rushing into them. Constable Pearce had a large smile on his face. It was just a few minutes past ten. They weren't too late all things considered. Frances stood up and smiled as they approached.

"Fancy running for office?" asked Pearce as he looked at Frances standing in the House of Lords as if she owned it.

"Not allowed to," she said.

"Really?" asked Pearce. "I thought you were allowed to stand for election to parliament for two years already?"

"Quite right, but we're still not allowed to become members of the House of Lords. We're stuck with the commoners in the House of Commons."

"Well, the good Lady Astor is there, she gave quite the speech earlier this year regarding drinking hours," said Husher.

Frances nodded.

"And the only woman in a den of men," she said, smiling, "though she wasn't the first woman elected to Parliament."

"You don't say," said Husher, feigning just the slightest of interest, though it appeared Pearce was more honestly intrigued. Frances shook her head.

"You might not like this, but Countess de Markievicz was elected for the seat of Dublin while in prison but hasn't taken it yet. You might remember her from her involvement with the Easter Uprising. She's a member of Sinn Fein."

Pearce nodded.

"You know, I do recall the name now that you've mentioned it."

Husher shrugged. He couldn't be bothered with politics generally and women's suffrage specifically.

"If I recall she's quite the firebrand," said Pearce, "calling on the court to carry out her death sentence when it was commuted on account of her sex they said."

Frances nodded.

"You know the case quite well."

"I try to keep abreast of the criminal world, what with the job I'm tasked with."

"Quite a harsh sentence I should think considering her crime," said Frances.

"Well, that's what treason will get you," said Pearce.

"That's a matter of which side you're fighting for," said Frances. "I should hardly think she felt she was fighting for England."

Pearce grinned.

"You're quite sympathetic to the Irishman's cause, aren't you?" he asked.

"I am sympathetic to a people who feel they have no voice in their own governance," retorted Frances.

Pearce continued to smile at her good naturedly.

"You should certainly run for office," he said.

"Not likely, I can't imagine I'd get many votes."

"Well," said Pearce. "You might just get mine."

Frances smiled at him as Husher coughed.

"I believe we are here not so much for politics as for the investigation of this murder we are on."

"Quite right, Inspector. Seeing as you both found it quite easily."

"We had help," said Pearce. "One of the Lords was walking out as we came in and he gave us great directions, didn't he, Inspector?"

Husher nodded his bulldog face.

"You might wonder why you found me in here, Inspector," said Frances.

Husher shrugged again.

"Not particularly." He looked around. "I don't see any offices."

Frances stepped aside, and turned around to look at the Woolsack's bench, then she looked back at the two policemen.

"This is the Woolsack's bench," she said.

"You don't say," said Pearce. He walked around her and sat down on it.

"Surprisingly uncomfortable," he said. "Needs some armrests at the very least."

Frances turned to face him and smiled at him.

"Yes, well I'm not sure that was ever the point. It was not developed for being a leisurely seat, but rather the epitome of British dominance of the wool trade."

"I don't understand."

"In the early thirteen hundreds," said Frances, "King Edward the 3rd decided that his Lord Chancellor whilst in council should sit on a bale of wool. Such a bale became known as the Woolsack."

"Why wool?" asked Pearce, genuinely interested.

"Because wool in the middle ages was of primary importance to England's economy and trade."

Pearce nodded, upturning his mouth.

"You're quite the history buff," he said.

"Well, Devlin," said Frances, "I believe that looking back at history gives us a lens from which to see the future."

Frances looked down at the red cushion.

"Just imagine the number of men who have sat on that very seat, and to think that perhaps the future might put a woman there too."

"Yes," said Husher, "I enjoy a history lesson as much as the next man, but how many of these sitting Lord Chancellors have been murdered."

Frances turned back to look at the Inspector. Pearce got up and walked back in front of Frances, standing to Husher's left.

"That's a very good question," said Frances, "and one that I don't have an answer to."

"Then perhaps we should stick with the task at hand," suggested Husher.

Frances nodded.

"Do you know where the Lord Chancellor's office is?" asked Husher.

"I will lead the way," said Frances.

Frances walked off behind the Woolsack and turned right, exiting the House of Lords and entering the narrow Peers' Private Corridor. On her left was the Peers' Robing Room and on the right the Judges' Court. At the end of the Peers' Private Corridor was the Chancellors' Corridor and across that was the lobby to the Lord Chancellor's Office. Frances led them in.

"Over on the left is the Lord Chancellor's Officers' Room, but on the right is probably our best bet. This is where the Baron Marphallow would have had his personal office."

She led them into the large room. It was the size of a large bedroom. At the one end of it was a large dark wood desk behind which sat a large wingback leather chair with studded brass buttons and tufted back. Opposite it was a large leather Chesterfield sofa with a similar fabric. The color of leather was similar to the dark wooden desk. An oiled dark walnut brown. In the middle of the sofa was a tufted foot rest in leather and matching the overall tone of the furniture. A low, large rectangular table was in front of that footstool and closer to the sofa than the desk.

In the middle of the floor between the desk and the sofa and upon which the table stood, was a large intricately designed Egyptian rug. On the left and right sides of the room as you faced the desk were bookshelves from waist height to ceiling. On the left side was a wet bar with counter along the side of the wall before the bookshelf started. On a silver tray were a couple of upturned cut lead crystal whisky tumblers and in a cut crystal carafe was what looked like whisky.

The room was clean and dust free. Very little clutter. The books were orderly and the bookshelves were full of them. Frances walked over to the desk and sat down in the large comfortable leather chair.

"Well then," said Husher, "what exactly are we looking for?" he asked, looking about the room as if he felt sorely out of place, which in fact he was.

"You're the detective, Inspector," said Lady Marmalade with a twinkle in her eye, "let's detect."

"Yes, let's just do that."

"I'm not sure what we're looking for, Inspector," continued Frances. "Could be anything, could be nothing. I'm going to look through his drawers and table to see if I can come up with anything. Perhaps the cabinets under the bookshelves might reveal something, or perhaps something is hidden between the books."

It was a long shot, but she wasn't certain they would find anything here in any event.

"I told you about the books I found in Lady Marphallow's home, didn't I?" asked Frances, knowing full well that she hadn't mentioned it at all.

Husher had moved across to the left bookshelf where the wet bar was. Pearce had started on the right. Husher looked over at Frances and shook his head.

"No, you didn't," he said.

"Well, she has her own room for one thing. Not big of course, but the master bedroom seems not to be shared between the married couple."

"I see," said Husher.

"Getting more to the point, Inspector," said Frances, "there were several books in her dressing table drawers. Two of them being Sherlock Holmes stories which I believe Paussage had inscribed and likely gifted them to her."

"What was the inscription?"

"I don't remember it perfectly but what I do remember was the important bits. He signed it with love and used only his first initial, S."

"Sinjin," said Husher.

Frances nodded.

"He also said how she was his Fleur de la Nuit."

"His night flower?"

"Well yes, that's the direct translation, but more importantly, Fleur de la Nuit is the most expensive perfume, made by the French perfume house Maison Tortue."

"Strange name for a perfumery," said Husher.

Pearce had a big grin on his face.

"And women spend a lot of money on this?" asked Pearce in comic doubt.

"Oh yes, yes indeed," said Frances. "It might surprise you to know that a bottle of Fleur de la Nuit is ten pounds, if it's on sale."

Pearce stopped what he was doing and looked at Frances with a frown.

"You must be joking."

"I never joke about perfumes," said Frances. "I have a bottle myself."

"So you think he gave her a bottle of this perfume?" asked Husher.

"Oh yes, almost certainly."

"Well," he continued, "that might suggest that they were having an affair but it doesn't mean he killed the Baron."

"Not in and of itself. Just wanted to keep you up to date."

"Thank you," said Husher as he continued to study the bookshelves.

On the desk in front of Frances were assorted papers, mostly bills that were coming up in parliament and other political correspondence. There was also a large ashtray, a big lighter the size of her hand and a humidor of Cuban cigars.

Frances opened up the first drawer on her right hand side. It was lockable but it had not been locked. It was a shallow drawer over a larger bigger drawer. Inside it were some coins from various European countries as well as English coins. There were some writing implements too and three telegrams. They were all from the same person. Frances took them out and looked at them. The top one was the newest so she read the oldest one first.

DOUBT OVER YESTERDAYS OFFICIAL UGLY LAWS STOP

OLIVER VILLENEUVE ERRS MORE EVERYDAY STOP

A

The second newest telegram read:

INTERESTINGLY, THE INCOMPETENT ROBSONS EGG ON FREDERICK STOP

HARANGUING IS MADDENING STOP

A

And the last one read:

KING IS LEAVING LATER STOP

HOW IS MORNING STOP

A

"This is interesting," said Frances.

Husher looked up.

"What is it?" he asked.

I have three telegrams here that seem to have come from Agnes Marphallow. It is easily determined from the post office and the telegram number, but I'm fairly certain they're from her. Husher came on over and took the telegrams from Frances.

"The first one is dated the 22nd, this second one the 24th and the last is from the 25th," he said.

Frances nodded. Pearce came on over and read the telegrams over Husher's shoulder.

"We only have the two from Lord Paussage, right?" he asked.

Frances nodded.

"I only found the two when I was looking through Lady Marphallow's dressing table."

"How did the Baron get ahold of these?" he asked.

"That's a good question, probably how we're finding them here. From snooping around in Lord Paussage's office," offered Frances. "Remember, that the Baron was looking to divorce her. You'll recall I found those legal documents in the Baron's room."

Husher nodded.

"Still, I don't see how these can help. Correspondence between the two doesn't seem to suggest a conspiracy to murder."

"Maybe it doesn't," said Frances. "But at the very least it adds more credence to the fact that they were likely having an affair, and as we both know, murder is a crime of passion very often."

Husher nodded.

"I'll keep these just in case," he said.

"Before you do, Inspector," said Frances, "can I just make a note of them."

Frances wrote down what they said in a small notebook she kept in her handbag, and then she returned them to Husher. They went back to exploring the parts of the office that they had been looking at before. Nothing else came to light that seemed relevant.

Before they left the House of Lords, Frances and Husher and Pearce popped into Lord Paussage's office, which he shared with another peer. As such, there wasn't much in there of note. Nothing personal that belonged to Paussage. Rather bland, boring and business only focused.

They stepped out onto the Old Palace Yard. Behind them was the River Thames, in front of them stood Westminster Abby, an important church mostly responsible for coronations and weddings. In fact, Princess Patricia of Connaught had been married just the year before to Captain the Honorable Alexander Ramsay in the Royal Peculiar as the church had become known in function. It was a wedding in February of 1919 which Frances had attended.

Frances stood facing the Abby with Husher to her left and Pearce to her right facing her. Over Husher's right shoulder she could see the statue of George the 5th, across the road, standing in full regal attire on a large white block.

"Would you like a ride back home?" asked Pearce.

Frances nodded.

"That would be lovely, thank you."

"Well, that didn't seem quite as hopeful as I had originally anticipated," said Husher in a dour tone.

"I disagree," said Frances, "I think it was just what we needed."

"I don't see how."

"Perhaps you could join me tomorrow at the Baron's home and I'll explain everything. Do you think you could ensure everyone is in attendance, including Lord Paussage?"

Husher looked at her with a raised eyebrow for a moment.

"You know who did it then, don't you?" asked Husher.

Frances nodded.

"We all know who did it, Inspector, the question remains, why was it done?"

"Do tell," said Husher.

Frances smiled slyly at him.

"I'll tell it all tomorrow. You have all the information that I have, Inspector," said Frances.

"I know why he did it," said Pearce.

Frances and Husher looked at him.

"Jealousy!" he exclaimed. "That's always the reason in instances like this."

"Quite right," said Frances.

"Only that's not the only thing that Frances will give us tomorrow Constable," said Husher. "Why did he do it that night? What drove him to it? Why not just continue with the affair? What's the rush?"

"I'll come to those answers by tomorrow too," said Pearce, smiling.

Husher turned to look at Lady Marmalade.

"Do you think you'll get a confession out of him?

That's what we really need," he said.

"I do, Inspector. I do," said Frances. "I believe I have all the clues needed for that. And even if they don't, I imagine any prosecutor in London will be happy with the evidence we've gathered."

"Good," said Husher as they walked off towards the police car. "What time then?"

"Let's say afternoon tea," said Frances. "Three tomorrow afternoon."

CHAPTER EIGHTEEN

Marphallow Home

FRANCES arrived at about ten minutes to three in the afternoon. Eric was with her. He wouldn't miss it for the world. She was going to weed out the murderer. He knew it and she knew it too. The evidence was strong and convincing, but Lady Marmalade was also hoping for a confession just to make the case stronger. And if things went well, she'd likely get her confession. She had her notes with her in her handbag and she was prepared to go with the flow of it as it went.

The police were already at the Baron's home. Frances saw their cars. There were two of them. It brought her great comfort as it meant that Inspector Husher had great confidence in her. As he had before. As he should.

Frances and Eric walked up to the home and knocked on the door. Humphrey opened it up and let them in. He smiled naturally at Frances.

"It's very good to see you, my Lady, my Lord," he said to both Frances and Eric.

Frances looked at him and smiled.

"It is very good to see you too," she said.

She offered him her hand and he shook it. She placed her other hand over top of his and looked him straight in the eye.

"Thank you for taking care of my fine," he said, somewhat low and in an embarrassed tone.

Frances nodded.

"Not at all, my dear man. And I hope that one day you will not have to hide your true self in the shadowy corners of our society."

He smiled sadly, and nodded. Frances walked into the home. Lord Marmalade shook his hand and exchanged pleasantries. Humphrey led them all into the living room. Agnes sat in a chair across from the sofa where her husband had been murdered. Lord Paussage sat in another chair across from her with another leather sofa between them. No one sat on the sofa that the Baron had been murdered on.

Lord Loughty sat on the sofa by himself. Frances was surprised to see him there, but it worked wonderfully well for her. He would make for a good red herring. Edith and Vera were not present. A couple of constables that Frances had not met were positioned in the room, and Inspector Husher and Pearce looked on at everyone from behind the Baron's leather couch. Husher nodded at Frances.

Frances walked over to where Husher and Pearce were. Eric went and sat down next to his friend, Larmer.

"You got here early," said Frances.

"The better to bring this investigation to an end," said Husher.

"Vera and Edith are in the kitchen I assume?" asked Frances.

Husher nodded.

"They're making scones and tea. I thought it better to keep them busy. Do you want to speak with them?"

Frances nodded.

"Edith is the last important piece I need to fit into this puzzle."

Husher nodded.

"It's the flour isn't it?"

Frances nodded.

"Would you come with me? Your stern demeanor might be just the trick I need to get what I want from her."

Husher nodded and she and Pearce walked with him off towards the kitchen. In the kitchen, Vera was just brining out some fresh baked scones from the oven. It smelt wonderful in there, with the fresh baked smell of those scones. The kettle was slowly coming to a boil on the stove. Vera saw them enter and smiled. Off to the right sat Edith, nervously fidgeting with her fingers and hands as she sat at the staff's table where Frances had met her the very first time she had come to the Marphallow home. The three of them walked up to her.

Edith startled and stood up from her chair. She tried to put a smile on her face, but it fell right off. She looked down at her hands. She had been chewing at her nails. She looked at them and then put her hands behind her back.

"Terrible habit, I know," she said nervously. Though Frances hadn't noticed before, for she hadn't chewed at them before.

"Do you know why we're here, dear?" said Frances, pleasantly.

Edith nodded.

"You're going to arrest the one who killed the Baron," she said, and then she blurted out. "It wasn't me."

Frances nodded.

"Yes, we know that, dear," she said. "But you are not entirely without guilt."

Vera placed the scones on a wire rack to cool, pretending not to pay any notice to them but of course pricking her ears to hear every word.

"I don't know what you mean," said Edith, looking at them briefly before looking away again.

"But you do," said Frances, "and we can do this civilly or we can take you down to the station in front of everyone here. Isn't that right, Inspector?"

Frances turned to look at him and he nodded gruffly.

"Unfortunately for you, Mrs. Edevane," he said in his gruff authoritarian tone, "we don't have a separate space for female suspects. You'll be put in with the men, unfortunately. Not the best place, I'm afraid, for a lady such as yourself."

Husher was lying, but Edith wouldn't have known any better. She swallowed and her face went pale.

"No, please don't, I don't think I could stand it," she said.

"Then make it easy on yourself," said Frances. "We know you put the money in Humphrey's overcoat. We saw the flour on your jacket cuff, so we know you had the key and you hid it in the flour. What we want to know is why you did it?"

"She made me do it," said Edith, looking between them and the table in front of her.

"Who?" asked Frances.

"Lady Marphallow," she said under her breath.

"Why?"

"I don't know, my Lady," said Edith. "She just told me to take the money and the key and put it in Humphrey's coat. She said that if I wanted to keep my job I'd do as I was told."

"So you went and took the money?" asked Husher.

"No, Inspector, Lady Marphallow handed the money and the key to me. The money was in the envelope so I took it out and stuffed it into Humphrey's pocket. And the key I tried to hide in the flour. I thought it wouldn't be found that way. I told her about it and she seemed quite pleased."

Frances nodded slowly.

"And what time was this?"

"Early, shortly after I arrived."

"And she came out to the kitchen and gave you the money then, whilst Vera was here?" asked Frances.

Edith shook her head.

"No, my Lady, that was the odd thing, she came right out the front door as I came walking by. This would have been just around eight thirty when I'm scheduled to be at work."

"I see, and did she seem out of sorts in any way?"

Edith looked down and furrowed her brow for a moment thinking. Then she nodded her head.

"Yes, she was. At first I thought she was upset with me."

"Why is that?"

"She came out quite flustered and looking agitated Lady Marmalade," said Edith, looking at Frances, "but then she thrust the envelope with money at me. She told me to put it in Humphrey's jacket and to hide the key."

"And you just did that?" asked Husher, interjecting.

Edith looked over at him, and shook her head.

"No, Inspector. I told her that was an awful lot of money and it would get Humphrey in trouble. She said there was already plenty of trouble with the money and that she couldn't keep all the staff on account of the Baron's financial troubles."

"Was that all?" asked Frances.

Edith shook her head again.

"No, she said that she knew that Humphrey was dissatisfied with his wages and that he was going to get what was coming to him. She would give him this as his severance. It sounded odd but I could see the logic to it, my Lady."

"What else did she say?" asked Frances.

"Only that if I spoke a word of this to anyone that it would be the end of my employment as a housekeeper anywhere in London. She was very firm when she said that. What could I do, my Lady? I need the job you see, I take care of my sick mother and there isn't much money to go around. Not lately."

"I understand," said Frances. "Doesn't sound like you've committed a crime." She looked over at the Inspector. "Inspector?"

Husher looked over at her and nodded.

"So long as we get your cooperation at court, Mrs. Edevane you'll have nothing to worry about."

Edith smiled a little at that and her whole face brightened.

"How did she look to you?" asked Frances. "You said she was flustered and agitated. How else would you describe her?"

"Yes, that's right. At first I thought she was upset at me. But she didn't sound any more upset than usual. What I mean to say is that she can be a very stern woman. No, my Lady, she looked to me like she hadn't slept in days. Her makeup didn't look fresh, her hair was a little disheveled and she had on the same clothes I'd seen her in on the day before. If I could be quite honest, she looked haggard."

"Very good," said Frances. "You've been quite helpful. You'll stay here with Vera and bring out the tea and scones when they're ready. You'll likely be unemployed come the end of the day but don't leave here under any circumstances until you've been dismissed by either myself, the Inspector or one of his constables."

Edith nodded. Frances turned to look at the Inspector.

"I think we have everything we need," she said.

"Agreed."

Pearce nodded his head and the three of them turned and walked back out of the kitchen and towards the living room where only Eric and Larmer spoke with each other. Everyone else was quiet. Frances came up and stood next to the side table which had some days before held the Baron's empty tumbler. Paussage looked up at the three of them.

"Could we get on with this," he said. "You do know that the House of Lords is in session and I'd like to make the tail end of it if possible."

Frances nodded at him.

"I do apologize, Lord Paussage, for this great inconvenience," said Frances. "It shouldn't take long and we'll have you on your way in no time."

Paussage nodded, very pleased with himself.

"But perhaps we could wait for just a few minutes until afternoon tea is served. It might be just what we need to soothe our spirits under such difficult circumstances."

"So long as it happens quickly, or I'll be on my way by myself," said Paussage.

The group of them sat in silence for just a couple of minutes until some commotion could be heard from the kitchen. Vera came out carrying a tray with a couple of teapots on it and enough teacups and saucers for everyone, including the police. Edith followed her with another tray with a dozen scones on it, still warm from the oven, clotted cream in a bowl and strawberry jam in another with some knives on the tray as well.

The two of them sat the trays down.

"The tea has been steeped," said Edith, and then she looked at Frances. "Should I pour for everyone, my Lady?" she asked.

"That is not necessary," said Agnes, visibly upset that she wasn't being addressed.

Edith bowed slightly and disappeared back into the kitchen with Vera. Humphrey stood off to the side like the good butler he was.

"The impertinence," said Agnes to no one in particular. "I should think she'll be fired by the end of the day."

Nobody said anything to that. Paussage leaned in

and poured himself some tea without offering anyone else first. He also took a scone, broke it in half and smeared both sides with cream and jam.

Eric leaned in after him and offered Agnes tea. She accepted so he poured her a cup. He offered his wife a cup and she took one too. There was no carafe of cream so Frances took milk and sugar in hers. She didn't take a scone. Eric offered his friend Larmer a cup of tea which was accepted and he offered the same to Pearce and Husher. He was turned down by Husher but Pearce as usual took him up on the offer.

Pearce, Loughty and Eric all took a scone too. After finishing his first half of the scone Paussage put the plate down next to his teacup and saucer on the side table on his right.

"Can we get on with this?" he said. "Why have we all been brought here?"

Frances took a sip of her tea and then put it on the side table next to her and the sofa where the Baron was murdered not quite a week before.

"We are here in the room where Baron Marphallow was murdered to confront the murderer and to bring justice," said Frances.

Everyone looked around at each other.

"So one of us here is alleged to have done it then?" asked Loughty, playing along.

Frances nodded.

"Yes, and I'm about to ferret that person out."

Paussage looked over at Agnes who looked back at

him.

"Murder, which you might or might not know is often a crime of passion. In my opinion I'm grateful for this, for once you have motive you often have the perpetrator," said Frances. "Wouldn't you agree, Inspector?"

Husher who had his arms crossed over his chest and his eyes steady on the group across from him nodded.

"I do. Almost always committed because of passion."

"And yet," continued Frances, "passion can come dressed in many different clothes. And this is where things get a little difficult. For example, we have many reasons and opportunities for why the Baron was murdered."

Frances looked around the room for a moment.

"The Baron, as almost everyone here knows, was the Lord Chancellor, the Woolsack of His Majesty's Government. He was a very powerful man, and like any powerful man, he made many enemies."

Frances looked over at her husband and smiled at him.

"My husband, also part of the opposition, was not particularly fond of the Baron's politics. But did that give him motive to murder the Baron?"

Frances looked around at everyone and picked up her teacup to take a sip. She raised her eyebrows.

"Anyone?" she asked.

"It could have given him motive if he disliked the man enough," said Loughty, enjoying playing devil's advocate.

"Quite right, but we did not investigate my husband, Lord Marmalade, because he was with me at home the night of the murder, as can be attested to by our children and our staff. But these are the sorts of questions one must ask oneself when investigating crimes of this sort."

Frances took another sip. The tea was delicious. She then put the teacup back down and looked at Loughty without irony.

"And you, Lord Loughty, had perhaps even more motive than my husband to murder the Baron."

"I beg your pardon," said Loughty feigning a slight, "I take umbrage at your accusations."

Paussage looked on with a small, sly smile on his face. Agnes too, looked quite relieved.

"Let me present the facts, Lord Loughty," continued Frances. "You were seen almost a fortnight ago in this very residence assaulting Lord Paussage."

"Well, yes, but he called me derogatory terms," said Loughty in protest, playing along.

"But you did assault him. More than that," said Frances, "you stormed out in anger, but not before threatening the Baron's life."

"I must take issue with your admonition," said Loughty. "I did not threaten the Baron directly, I only suggested that because of his unwillingness to sit down with the IRM that it would be the end of him."

"I was there, Larmer," said Paussage, feeling quite proud of himself, "and I heard what I heard." He turned to Frances. "I will swear an oath as to what I heard."

Frances smiled at him and nodded.

"That won't be necessary," she said. "We have more than enough evidence on the murderer."

"Good," said Paussage, obviously happy with himself. He picked up his plate and started to eat the second half of his scone.

"In fact," said Frances, "police picked up three ne'er do wells across from this very home who, the night of the Baron's murder, give eyewitness testimony to seeing you, Lord Loughty, attend at the Baron's home at between ten fifteen and ten twenty."

"Untrue," exclaimed Loughty. "Who were these men?"

"They are known members of the IRM," said Frances.

"Ah ha," said Loughty, enjoying the act. "And these are the people you will call upon in court to swear that they saw me enter the Baron's home and murder him. Men who are known cheats and liars."

"Works for me," said Paussage through a mouthful of scone.

"Unfortunately," said Frances. "These eyewitnesses don't put you entering the home, but rather leaving just after having arrived."

"Exactly," said Loughty, "because I did not attend the Baron's home to murder him, but rather to apologize."

Paussage nodded his head sarcastically.

"Right, you probably slipped round the back to murder him," he said.

Loughty gave him a stern look, but he knew the man was a goner. So he bit his tongue and grimaced.

"I'm afraid not," said Frances. "The witnesses saw Lord Loughty leave. We have no further evidence that Larmer was involved."

Paussage shrugged and finished his scone, put the plate on the side table and then sipped on tea. Frances took a moment to take a drink too. Pearce stood just slightly behind her enjoying his tea and the show. On the other side, also slightly behind Frances, stood Husher with his arms folded in front of him. He stood solid and stolid as a granite statue.

"That led me to look closer to home as to who might have a motive," said Frances. "And I recall speaking with the butler, Mr. Spilligan, the morning of the murder and you," said Frances, turning to face him, "were belligerent with me and unhappy with your employers."

"But I didn't kill him," said Humphrey, unsure of whether Frances had genuine renewed interest in him or not. Frances winked at him so that only he could see.

"Yes, that is what you told me at the time. And then

when we came inside to look into your locker you went to check on Lady Marphallow, only you didn't. You ran like a guilty man."

Humphrey hung his head in shame.

"But I did not kill him," he said softly. He had seen the wink and was playing along.

"You never can trust hired help," said Agnes, looking on at Humphrey. He looked up at her, wanting to say something, but bit his lip instead. Even under these circumstances, if he wanted to find further employment as a butler, he had to remain calm and unperturbed.

"Yes, it did seem quite suspicious," said Frances, "especially since we then found the stolen money in his jacket pocket."

Frances looked over at Agnes. She looked up in feigned surprise. Then she looked at Humphrey.

"You are fired, Mr. Spilligan. Go on, get going. Take your things and leave, and I will make sure you never find work as a butler in this city again."

Agnes looked around quite pleased with herself. Humphrey didn't move.

"What are you waiting for?" she asked.

"If you don't mind, dear," said Frances, looking at Agnes, "I'd rather everyone stay until the murderer has been taken into custody."

Agnes nodded.

"Well, what are you waiting for? He clearly did it. If he could take the money and run off then he must have done it."

"It would seem so," said Frances, "except that he didn't."

"How can you be so certain?" asked Agnes.

"For several reasons," she said. "He was seen leaving this home at around ten by our witnesses, and when we caught up with him and interrogated him, he had an alibi as to where he was and why he ran on the morning of your husband's murder."

"Well, I for one would love to know what that alibi is," said Agnes. "As his employer I am entitled to this information."

"Except that you are not his employer as you just fired him," said Frances. "In any event, that's confidential information and will only be released if Mr. Spilligan's testimony is required in court, which I highly doubt. The police are content with the information provided and it takes him off the list of suspects."

"The outrage," said Paussage. "The man stole the money and he's off the hook. Perhaps he didn't murder the Baron, but the theft of a hundred pounds is surely no small matter."

Frances nodded.

"You are quite correct, Sinjin, and how did you know how much money was stolen?"

Paussage's face went flushed.

"I... I don't... I am merely speculating... I imagine the Baron in his situation might keep around that much money in the home."

Paussage looked away and took his teacup. He brought it to his lips with hands that trembled ever so slightly, but which Frances took note of.

"No matter," said Frances, "Mr. Spilligan didn't steal the money. He left the Friday evening at around ten and nobody has him having stolen it then. He was late coming into work on the Saturday morning. So late in fact, that he hardly had the time to steal the money then."

"He must have found a way," said Agnes.

Frances shook her head.

"No, I'm afraid not. There was a conspiracy to have it look like he stole the money."

"Ha," said Agnes, tossing her head back, "that sounds ridiculous."

"Well, we found out that Mrs. Edevane placed the money in Mr. Spilligan's pocket to make it look like he stole it."

Agnes and Paussage fell silent. Loughty took his opportunity.

"But why would she steal it to make it look like he took it. That makes absolutely no sense. She'd be better off just taking it for herself," said Loughty, looking around and pretending to be quite confused.

"You're quite right, Larmer, it would make greater sense for Mrs. Edevane to take the money rather than to put it on Mr. Spilligan. Unless..."

Frances paused for good measure.

"Unless she had a good reason to do so. But it would have to mean that the value was greater than the hundred pounds she'd be giving up by framing Mr. Spilligan."

Loughty nodded and turned up his mouth in agreement.

"Yes, that would make sense," he said, "but what could that reason be for her to take such a high risk position?"

"I'm glad you asked," said Frances. She picked up her teacup and took a sip and then looked around the room. Paussage and Lady Marphallow didn't meet her gaze.

"Her employer forced her to do it," said Frances, keeping an eye on Agnes.

"This is outrageous," said Agnes. "I will not stand to hear these baseless allegations against me." Then she looked towards the kitchen. "And you're fired too, Mrs. Edevane," she shrieked.

"Calm down," said Frances.

"Calm down. Calm down. You want me to calm down when you hurl such vitriolic allegations at me? You take the word of a commoner over me?"

"I take the word of one commoner over another," said Frances.

"And what is that supposed to mean?" asked Agnes, her cheeks still hot with anger.

"It means that you were a commoner once, if you wish to use that term as a slight, before you married the Baron for his money."

Agnes looked over at Paussage.

"Please do something, Sinjin, these insults are outrageous."

"Why yes... I... this is outrageous. I think we should be off," said Lord Paussage, trying his best to get up out of his chair, but not managing it as quickly as he might have liked, with his heft getting in the way.

"You'll stay right where you are," exclaimed Husher, in a deep and authoritarian voice that seemed to beat Paussage back into his chair and bring a deadly quiet over the room. Frances turned towards the Inspector and smiled at him.

"Thank you, Inspector."

"Well, you have no proof that I gave Edith the money," said Agnes.

"You're quite correct, though with what we do have, I'm certain we won't need that proof."

"I'd like to know who did it," said Loughty, starting to really have fun with the hot seats that Agnes and Sinjin were in. "The suspense is killing me. No pun intended."

It was a poor joke that no one laughed at.

"Yes, we should get right down to brass tacks, I should think," said Frances. "Lady Agnes Marphallow and Lord Sinjin Paussage conspired to murder Baron Christopher Marphallow."

"Utter nonsense," said Paussage, "there were no prints on the letter opener."

Frances smiled at him. Lord Paussage looked at her for a moment unknowingly, and then slowly he realized what he had just said. His face went pale, and he looked away. Agnes looked at him with a furrowed and very worried brow.

"I rest my case," said Frances. "How would you know, a, the murder weapon, and b, that it was wiped clean of prints?"

"Damn you, Sinjin," said Agnes.

Paussage said nothing. He remained mute as if the cat had got ahold of his tongue.

"That's good enough for me," said Husher. He turned to nod at his Constables. "Take them to the Yard."

"Wait, wait, please," said Lord Loughty, "I want to know how you knew."

"Yes, and I would like to know too, darling," said Eric.

Husher nodded at the Constables and they stepped back to their previous positions. Frances nodded and smiled.

"The first clue was when I visited with Agnes in the dining room. She looked terrible. But I thought that she was just quite upset. I have since learned that she did not sleep that night, and in fact, she was wearing the same clothes she had on the night before, according to the housekeeper Edith, who saw her early on Saturday morning and remarked to me how poorly Agnes looked as if she had been up all night."

Eric and Larmer nodded in unison.

"And then along with that, I noticed that the Baron had been drugged. Although Agnes had informed me that she and the Baron took sleeping aids each evening and that she gave the Baron his. However, I noticed two envelopes of Medinal just under the couch near the Baron and in Agnes' room there was no sign that she had slept in the bed nor was there any indication that the cup she had up there had once held said Medinal. For unlike the Baron's tumbler which clearly had powdered residue, hers did not."

"Very good, very good indeed," said Loughty. "So, that certainly sounds suspicious but it doesn't appear that it would indicate murder."

"No," said Frances, "you're quite right. Agnes might have given the Baron a double dose if he had asked for it, but then why lie to me? In any event, it brought suspicion upon her."

"But there were a couple of other items I found in the Baron's room and then in Agnes' room. In the Baron's room were divorce documents."

Agnes looked up at Frances with anger and hatred hot in her eyes.

"You have no idea what it's like to claw your way to the top only to have the person you married, whom you put up with for years toss you aside like a used napkin."

"I'll get to the reasons as to why you killed him in a bit," said Frances. "But I think thou doth protest too much."

Larmer slapped his leg. This was too much fun.

"What did you find in Lady Marphallow's room?"

"Well," said Frances, "it was fairly common knowledge that Lady Marphallow was courting several men. One of whom was Lord Paussage."

Lord Paussage looked over at Agnes.

"What?" he said, half in disbelief.

"Not true," she said to him, looking coy.

"Quite true I'm afraid, Sinjin. You've been manipulated. It has come to our attention that Lady Marphallow was familiar with at least one other Lord, who's name right now is unimportant."

Lord Paussage shook his head in disgust, finding the higher ground a bit slippery.

"Who said such lies?" asked Agnes.

"Your staff dear, are quite aware of your infidelities," said Frances, "but so is Lord Loughty. You really ought to be more discreet. But then I suppose someone from your station wouldn't know any better. All you are interested in is finding another man to marry after nearly exhausting the Baron's wealth."

"That is patently false," said Agnes, "the Baron wasted his own money."

"Quite true, with your help of course, and what little he did have left, he wanted to keep from you and that was why he was going to divorce you. And I believe you knew."

"Of course I knew," said Agnes, "that lily-livered

man was a coward. I mean you saw him, the only reason I married him was for his money, which it turned out he used to spend on horses and other gambling habits of his. I wasn't going to let him take everything away from me."

Then she turned and looked over at Lord Paussage.

"If you knew what you were doing, we could have been together with more money than we both could have dreamed of. But instead you're a bumbling buffoon."

"I told you it was a bad idea from the beginning," said Paussage, "but it is so much easier to get someone else to do the dirty work for you, isn't it?"

"I've heard enough," said Husher. "If you don't mind I'll take them in, now that they've as much as confessed."

"Please, Inspector," said Loughty, "I really would love to hear how Frances put it all together."

Frances looked at the Inspector and nodded. He nodded gruffly in return.

"So I knew that knowing about the divorce, Agnes was wont to do something drastic. That gave me motive. But I needed something else. Something that gave evidence to the fact that she was a disloyal woman. I had plenty of hearsay, but I wanted something meatier."

"And did you get it?" asked Eric.

Frances nodded.

"I did. In Agnes' room was a bottle of Fleur de la

Nuit. The world's most expensive perfume. It could have been a gift from her husband, but it wasn't. And I know this because in one the drawers of the dressing table were a couple of Sherlock Holmes' stories. Inside the one was this inscription."

Frances opened up her handbag and took our her notebook to read the passage.

"'My Darling,

Your beauty is a greater mystery than Sherlock could ever solve. I am entranced by your beauty and elegance. You are my Fleur de la Nuit.

All love,

S'

Clearly from Lord Sinjin Paussage."

"Brilliant," said Larmer. "That confirms the affair they were having but what about the murder?"

Frances nodded.

"There were also two telegrams also signed by 'S'. The earlier one," said Frances looking at her notes, "was from the 23rd of November. It read: I WILL INVESTIGATE LEGAL LIABILITIES STOP AND LOOK WHERE ANGRY YORKSHIREMEN SIT STOP S."

Frances looked up at her audience. They were entranced.

"The second one was from the 26th. It read: IN WINTER IT LOOKS LOVELY STOP S."

Loughty frowned at her.

"Yes," she said, "quite odd telegrams. The first one

might be related to some sort of political issue, but the second one seems strange, without context."

Loughty nodded.

"It gives no indication of murder," he said.

"Not at first glance," she said, "but when you have all the telegrams associated with these in order it starts to look more interesting."

"And where are the others from this conversation?" asked Loughty.

"We found the others in the Lord Chancellor's room at the House of Lords," said Frances, looking over at Paussage.

"So that's where they went," said Paussage, looking dejected.

"Imbecile," said Agnes. "I told you not to keep them in your office."

He looked over at her.

"It seemed a good place at the time. I was meaning to get rid of them," he said. "But I kept them, because they were from you. I loved you. I'd have done anything for you."

Agnes shook her head at him in disgust.

"Well, it appears you did do just about anything for her," said Frances, "including murder."

Lord Paussage looked down. There was no use denying it now. But he had no fight left in him. He hadn't wanted to do it, but she'd made him feel like it was the only way they could be together. In fact, she'd had to help him, he found the actual act nauseating.

Loughty looked back at Frances having studied the now dejected Paussage who held no higher ground, who was no longer the proud and contemptible man he had known just a few short weeks ago.

"And what did these other telegrams say?" he asked.

Frances looked over at him and nodded, after putting down her teacup which she had taken a sip of. The tea was getting cold.

"It might be better if I read them in order," she said.

She looked through her notebook and found what she needed.

"This first one was from Agnes, dated the 22nd. DOUBT OVER YESTERDAYS OFFICIAL UGLY LAWS STOP OLIVER VILLENEUVE ERRS MORE EVERYDAY STOP A. Then there was that one from Sinjin dated the 23rd."

"Can you read it again?" asked Loughty, trying to tease out the puzzle.

Frances nodded.

"I WILL INVESTIGATE LEGAL LIABILITIES STOP AND LOOK WHERE ANGRY YORKSHIREMEN SIT STOP S."

Loughty frowned.

"I suppose it could have to do with some political issue, but the language is a bit odd, and I know of no such Oliver Villeneuve."

Loughty looked over at Eric. Eric shrugged.

"I quite agree," he said. "Nothing in those telegrams

rings a bell for me. As for the Yorkshiremen, that's odd without context. We have Yorkshiremen in the House but it seems quite cryptic."

"That's because it is," said Frances. "Let me continue with the rest."

Loughty nodded.

"The next one is also from Agnes and dated the 24th. INTERESTINGLY, THE INCOMPETENT ROBSONS EGG ON FREDERICK STOP HARANGUING IS MADDENING STOP A."

"I see," said a confused Loughty.

"Then there is a last one from Agnes dated the 25th. KING IS LEAVING LATER STOP HOW IS MORNING STOP A."

"And that's it?" asked Loughty.

"No, there was the last one I read earlier from Sinjin dated the 26th. IN WINTER IT LOOKS LOVELY STOP S."

"I must say, I can't make heads or tails of it," said Loughty, looking around.

"That's because they were private love letters between the two of us," said Agnes, trying to derail the truth.

"Private they were," said Frances, "but love letters they were not. They were cryptic instructions between the two of you regarding the Baron."

Agnes looked away and didn't say anything to her. Loughty was still quite confused.

"How on earth do you get that from these very odd telegrams?" he asked.

"Well," said Frances, "that was the key. They seemed oddly written and didn't quite make sense even when I had them together and tried to tease out the true meaning from them. Agnes would have no need, nor interest in any political issue that she would need or be privy to discussing with Sinjin. So the only telegrams I could foresee between the two of them should likely be about clandestine meetings of their illicit affair. But that didn't quite seem the case from the language nor tone of the telegrams."

Loughty nodded.

"So I started to look at the words specifically, and then I saw exactly what they were about."

"Go on, I'm still not with you," said Loughty.

"Well," said Frances. "A murder that hopes to remain unsolved should not offer up evidence. The planning should leave no trace at the very least."

Frances looked at her notebook and then at Loughty.

"On with it, you're teasing me, Fran," he said good naturedly.

"It was in the words. Specifically it was the first letter of each word that was trying to convey the real message of the telegrams. So for example. The first telegram was from Agnes on the 22nd and read: DOUBT OVER YESTERDAYS OFFICIAL UGLY LAWS STOP OLIVER VILLENEUVE ERRS MORE EVERYDAY

STOP A. Except for the STOP which is not considered part of the telegram as you'll know, the actual telegram then reads: DO YOU LOVE ME, when taking just the first letter of each word."

"Good lord," said Loughty, "so that was their scheme to plan and commit the murder? Read the other ones so I can find the rest of the hidden meanings."

Frances smiled at him. Loughty was quite excited by all of this.

"You'll notice that there is a theme to these telegrams. A question is answered by a response. So Agnes has asked DO YOU LOVE ME? And the next telegram is from Lord Paussage and responds: I WILL INVESTIGATE LEGAL LIABILITIES STOP AND LOOK WHERE ANGRY YORKSHIREMEN SIT STOP S. This was on the 23rd. What does it say?" asked Frances.

Loughty looked up for a moment trying to tease out the meaning. His lips moved silently as he spoke the lines again, focusing on the first letter of each word.

"I WILL ALWAYS," said Loughty, looking at Frances.

Frances nodded.

"I see," said Loughty, "but these two just show their alleged love for one another?"

Frances nodded again.

"Quite right," she said. "Agnes is trying to tease out Lord Paussage's loyalty for her and how much she might be able to manipulate him. You must understand, Larm, I doubt this was the only conversation the two of them had regarding murdering the Baron. I'm sure they would have spoken about it in person, but this is the only evidence we have of it in conversation."

"Right," he said, "so the other telegrams must be about the actual deed?"

"Quite right," said Frances. "Here's the next telegram in order. Written by Agnes on the 25th: INTERESTINGLY, THE INCOMPETENT ROBSONS EGG ON FREDERICK STOP HARANGUING IS MADDENING STOP A."

Frances looked up from her notebook. Loughty was nodding his head.

"And then she writes him again on the 25th. The last telegram from her that we have: KING IS LEAVING LATER STOP HOW IS MORNING STOP A. And then the very last telegram in the series is a response from Lord Paussage on the 26th: IN WINTER IT LOOKS LOVELY STOP S."

Frances folded her notebook in half and looked up at the crowd. Agnes and Sinjin sat dejected with heavy heads looking towards the floor.

"I TIRE OF HIM, she said," said Loughty. "And then, KILL HIM, to which Sinjin responds, I WILL. This is terribly fun, in a macabre sort of way."

He grinned from ear to ear, and looked over to Paussage.

"Cat got your tongue?" he asked.

Paussage looked up, his face flushed again in anger.

"You don't know what it's like to have found the woman you're in love with. You'd do anything for her. Besides you didn't like the Baron anyway."

"I still wouldn't have murdered the man," said Loughty.

"There were many reasons he needed to go. Not the least of which was his softening stance on the mick problem."

Loughty smiled at the insult. It was water off a duck's back. Paussage would find the justice he deserved, and that was a delicious dish served right up by his friend and her husband, Lord and Lady Marmalade.

"Except you couldn't keep your big fat mouth shut," said Agnes. "Not only that, I had to finish it off. That coward," she said, pointing a finger at Paussage, "got squeamish after putting the knife in his chest. I had to make sure to finish the half hearted job you did."

Frances turned towards the Inspector.

"I should think we've all heard enough."

"Agreed," he said, and he nodded at his constables.

CHAPTER NINETEEN

Marphallow Home

OUTSIDE in the front garden they all stood watching Agnes and Sinjin put into two separate police cars. Husher got into the front one with one of the constables. Pearce came up to Lady Marmalade.

"That was good work," he said, offering his hand.

"Not at all," she replied, "you would have had them in any event."

"And yet, it was, dare I say, more fun."

He grinned at her, and turned to leave.

"Until next time," he said, waving his hand in the air as he walked off.

"Sadly, there is always a next time," she said softly after him.

Pearce got into the second police car and the two cars drove off. Everyone watched them disappear down the street. Bishops Avenue was once again quiet, majestic and posh. Humphrey stood stoically behind them all with his hands clasped behind his back. Edith and Vera hugged each other sadly. For their collegial friendship though strained at points was coming to an end. Humphrey was perhaps less concerned so long as Frances would honor her word to put in a good word for him. He was sure that as a reference, finding another butlering position would not be difficult, even under these difficult times. And he was right.

"Well," said Loughty, "I suppose the Baron's sister is on her way from Australia to take care of the estate."

Frances and Eric nodded.

"Poor woman," said Eric.

Loughty turned to look at him.

"I wouldn't say that. I don't think they've been particularly close for some years. I've never heard him mention her often."

Eric turned around and took in the majestic home. He smiled sadly.

"Such a shame," he said.

"What's that, darling?" asked Frances, turning to see what he was looking at.

"A home," said Eric, holding his hand out towards the house, "should be a place of peace and of goodwill. And yet, this old home has seen recent misery. You wonder if it'll ever forget."

Frances put her hand through her husband's elbow and smiled towards the home, which stood squat and uncomplaining if not a little dour.

"I am sure," said Frances, "in time, with new

owners, this house will remember these events as if they were a long lost bad dream. A distant memory."

Eric turned and looked down at his wife and smiled. He kissed her on the forehead.

"Politics can be deadly," he said, "at least you know that about war."

Frances looked onward at the house.

"Politics of the heart are perhaps more so."

The two of them turned around again and looked out at the open street. It was a quiet street, without a soul out and about on it. Everyone was huddled up in their homes or perhaps at work, each man seeking his own counsel. This murder of the Baron however, was an aberration on Bishops Avenue and it was something that would likely stir the minds of the next generation of children who grew up in these opulent houses, amongst families that thought the trappings of wealth and success were sure to insulate them from such horrors.

And yet the vices and viciousness of men knows no boundaries. It seeks victims indiscriminately and it metes its wrath upon all. Just like death comes a-calling for every man and woman, so to do the savage beasts within unbridled men's passions.

"My Sisyphean task complete," said Frances, "I seek rest amongst the kind and kindred souls of my family."

"Come, my weary companion, let us be off to find solace and goodliness in our fellow men. And let this charity start at home," said Eric.

And he led Frances towards the car and away from the blighted Bishops Avenue which had never known such atrocity and, God willing, never would again.